A Candlelight Ecstasy Romance ®

"YOU DON'T GIVE UP, DO YOU?

"Ward, we can't go back. The time we spent together was . . . special, but it's over. What is it you want from me?"

When a slow smile spread across his face, Stacy's temper exploded. "Enough! We work together and that's all—*understand*? Why won't you accept that?"

"Because it's not true. And you know it too. I wanted you then and I want you now—and this time there's no safe Don Kemble to run to. Your position at the *Monitor* has nothing to do with our relationship."

"But there *isn't* any relationship! How can I make you see that?" she cried.

In answer, he closed the distance between them and towered over her. His lips slid over hers, sending bright darts of pleasure to the slowly tightening spring at the core of her body. The old familiar maelstrom began to brew inside her, pulling at her very sense of being, drawing her down into oblivion, into its seductive, mindless pool of pure sensation.

A CANDLELIGHT ECSTASY ROMANCE ®

A LASTING IMAGE

Julia Howard

A CANDLELIGHT ECSTASY ROMANCE ®

Published by
Dell Publishing Co., Inc.
1 Dag Hammarskjold Plaza
New York, New York 10017

Dell ® TM 681510, Dell Publishing Co., Inc.
Candlelight Ecstasy Romance®, 1,203,540, is a registered
trademark of Dell Publishing Co., Inc.,
New York, New York.

ISBN: 0-440-14723-9

Printed in the United States of America
First printing—December 1983

To Mom and Papa,
for their love and support,
and, of course,
to Bill

To Our Readers:

We have been delighted with your enthusiastic response to Candlelight Ecstasy Romances®, and we thank you for the interest you have shown in this exciting series.

In the upcoming months we will continue to present the distinctive sensuous love stories you have come to expect only from Ecstasy. We look forward to bringing you many more books from your favorite authors and also the very finest work from new authors of contemporary romantic fiction.

As always, we are striving to present the unique, absorbing love stories that you enjoy most—books that are more than ordinary romance.

Your suggestions and comments are always welcome. Please write to us at the address below.

Sincerely,

The Editors
Candlelight Romances
1 Dag Hammarskjold Plaza
New York, New York 10017

CHAPTER ONE

"Mr. Johnson? When does the *Evening Monitor* arrive?" Stacy Kemble asked, entering the old-fashioned drugstore. She automatically headed for the large glass jars of nuts lining the counter and began measuring out her habitual quarter pound of pistachios.

A boy's voice answered her from the doorway before the store's genial proprietor, occupied with another customer, could reply.

"Here, miss, just puttin' 'em in the bin now," he said in a thin, eager voice. "Somethin' important in it?"

Laughing, she shook her dark chestnut curls in denial. "No, I'm afraid not. Only my article about something that happened in Sacramento. I just got back."

She took the paper he held out to her and, after paying Mr. Johnson for her purchases, leaned against the counter, dipping her hand into the plastic bag. The pistachio opened easily and she popped it into her mouth with a quick flick of her wrist. She rolled the nut around on her tongue until she couldn't wait any longer, then sank her teeth into its yielding green flesh.

"It's not much of a reward, but here's to a job well done," she murmured to herself, savoring the nut's rich flavor.

Barely giving the rest of Wednesday's front page a glance, she started to read her story. But she stopped abruptly, a picture on the bottom half of the page drawing her eyes from the Sacramento story. Her face paled under its light tan.

"No!" she cried in a stunned whisper.

"You a reporter or somethin'?" the boy asked, impressed.

"Yes, yes, I'm a reporter," she answered absently, her hazel eyes clouding with concern at the announcement blaring across the bottom half of the front page.

"This is terrible!" she said, her motorcycle helmet falling to the floor with a clunk. "He can't show up now!"

Edward Fallbrook, the new editor of the *Monitor*! No, it couldn't be . . .

The newspaper's dull gray print couldn't hide the appeal in his eyes. All those memories she'd tried so hard to suppress came back to her as his face smiled out from the paper.

"Oh, Robbie, why did you have to retire now?" she whispered.

Mr. Johnson finished with his customer and went around behind the counter. "Is something wrong?" he asked gently.

"No!" she said, startled. "No. I guess I should accept that stories dictated over the phone usually get a little scrambled." She hated the fib, but how could she explain her turmoil? That she'd had an affair with Ward five years ago, then had married someone else?

The rotund man patted her shoulder ineffectually. "These things happen, you know." He glanced at the open paper on the counter.

"That the new editor? Clancy Shaw was in here earlier

and said they'd announced this guy Fallbrook will be taking over from Mr. Roberts at the *Monitor*. Do you know when he'll be arriving?" he asked innocently.

The bell on the front door announced a customer's arrival and Mr. Johnson left her to deal with the news in private. She caught her breath at the thought of seeing Ward daily at the *Monitor*. It had been so long. . . . For all she knew he could even have gotten married by now. He could have children! What would his wife be like? Would his children have his wizard's eyes? A knot formed in the pit of her stomach.

The proprietor returned. "Feeling better now?" he asked, patting her shoulder again.

"I don't know when this Fallbrook is supposed to arrive," she said evenly. "I didn't even know they'd hired someone to fill Robbie's place."

"You mean they didn't tell you this young man would be the new editor? Seems they could at least tell their own reporters."

Stacy thought exactly the same thing. "No, I knew Mr. Roberts was planning to retire, but that's *all* I knew. But I'm sure Fallbrook is very well qualified," she added defensively. He should be; when she'd known him, he'd been one of the best reporters in the state of California.

"Yes, of course, Mrs. Kemble. But what about . . ." he began.

"I'm sorry, Mr. Johnson, but I really have to go now. I just got back from Sacramento and I need to call in," Stacy said desperately, hoping the half lie would go undetected. The man was a dear, but right now she didn't feel like talking.

"Well, see you later." The bell on the door clanged

loudly, but not loud enough to drown the questions raging through her brain.

The white motorcycle hummed peacefully as she aimed it toward home, but it was the only thing peaceful around her. In her mind she saw Ward's face as it was the last time she'd seen him; his gray eyes had been nearly black with anger as he had towered over her. Even the memory of that confrontation made her nerves jangle with reaction. He'd been furious and demanding then—furious at her for breaking off their intense relationship and demanding that she tell him why she was marrying Don Kemble. She'd walked out without giving him an answer.

Parking the bike in her garage, she realized that becoming distraught over an old boyfriend showing up suddenly would do her no good at all. Her mind balked at using such a tame word as *boyfriend;* surely there was a different term to describe the Ward Fallbrooks of the world. She'd have to work with him, yes, but that's all she'd be doing with him! Their relationship would be kept strictly professional. She'd see to that.

Nearing the front door, her firm step reinforced that decision and she walked up the wooden stairs, unconsciously avoiding the spot where it would creak and start the neighbor's dog barking.

The dying light from the autumn sunset streamed through the screen door as Stacy entered, and it caught the red highlights in her hair as she shook out her long curls to restore their bounce; the helmet always crushed her hair.

She threw the paper onto the hallway table. Ward's picture stared out at her from the front page and she flipped the newspaper over with a quick angry movement, ignoring the frustration writhing inside her.

12

After hanging her helmet on the end of the banister, she went upstairs to her bedroom. The walls of the room were covered with photographs she'd shot and printed and she could feel herself relax under their benign influence. Walking to the desk in the corner, she pulled her telephone out from under a stack of proof sheets and punched the number for the *Evening Monitor.*

"*Monitor,* night desk," a voice answered over the noise of a police scanner. The noise faded suddenly as it was turned down.

"Hi, Mel. This is Stacy. Can you answer a couple of questions about this Fallbrook?" she asked.

"That was a great story from Sacto, Stace," Melody Atkins said.

"Thanks."

"What was it you wanted to know about this guy? Gorgeous, isn't he? Single too. I'm not going to mind having him around the newsroom at all!" the woman said, causing Stacy to feel a painful kind of impatience and a touch of relief she refused to acknowledge.

"But I really don't know much more than what was in the paper," Melody went on. "Meeves just came into the newsroom this afternoon and announced Fallbrook had been hired as the new editor. Robbie had a big smile on his face, so I suppose he knew. You've seen the paper, haven't you?"

"Sure. But why the sudden announcement? We all knew Robbie was retiring, but I didn't hear a squeak about this new editor before I left." Stacy had to sit down; her knees were shaking worse than her voice.

"We were all caught by surprise—don't know why it was hush-hush. I guess our beloved publisher was just indulging his penchant for drama."

13

Stacy took a deep breath for courage and asked, "When do you expect him to show up?"

"Hmmm, I think I heard Robbie say he was going fishing up in the Sierra a week from this coming Monday, so that'd be my guess. Don't know for sure though."

Stacy forced a laugh and said, "That sounds like Robbie." Her own vacation was starting at the end of the week, so she'd have plenty of time before he showed up. Willing her voice not to reveal the relief she felt, she added, "Thanks for the info, Mel. I'll see you tomorrow."

"Sure thing, Stace," the woman's voice answered. "Oh, I just remembered—Meeves said something about Fallbrook stopping by the newsroom later this week. I think he said Fallbrook wanted to get acquainted with the staff before he took over. Adios."

Pressure in her chest told Stacy that she'd forgotten to breathe. Taking a deep lungful of air, she belatedly hung up the phone and sat back in her chair. *Later this week!* She wasn't even going to get the week's reprieve she'd counted on.

She didn't see the pile of darkroom notes in front of her as she worried about the inevitable meeting with Ward. Her fingers idly fanned the stack and she briefly considered transferring the notes to the proofsheets—anything to get her mind off him. But that dull, much-needed task was pushed aside; she knew she couldn't concentrate tonight.

Was she afraid of meeting him again after so long? But she knew the fluttering in her heart wasn't fear. And that made her more upset than ever.

The alarm sounded rudely in the darkness of the early

14

morning. Coming out of a deep sleep, Stacy groggily beat at the clock until a lucky hit managed to turn it off.

A half-hour later, dressed in a classically tailored dark-brown pants suit, she downed a quick breakfast of toast and coffee. With her red motorcycle helmet tucked under one arm, she went out to the garage.

Her 650 BMW came to life with a satisfying roar. The bike was a dream to ride and she smiled as she eased it out onto the street, its headlight shining out into the predawn stillness.

Fifteen minutes later, carrying her helmet by its chin strap, she walked into the lobby of the *Evening Monitor*.

"Stacy!" a young woman cried with a curious mixture of worry and relief.

"What's wrong, Margaret?" Stacy asked, her voice sounding overly sharp to her ears. Margaret, the newsroom assistant, was difficult to take when it wasn't early in the morning, and right now Stacy had to struggle to remain civil.

"Mr. Roberts wants to see you right away."

Why did the girl have to make everything sound like a three-alarm fire? And why would Robbie want to see her? Stacy fought a rising feeling of panic and followed the stubby young woman to the back of the newsroom.

"He's in his office," Margaret said, opening the door.

She heard the door click shut behind her and a feeling of dread came over her.

Her heart stopped as she breathed in the telltale aroma of cigars that filled the room, a scent totally unlike that of the stale cigarette smoke that usually filled the newsroom.

Did he still smoke the same kind of cigar? A chuckle told her she'd unconsciously spoken out loud.

She whirled around. A tall lean man was resting nonchalantly against the credenza, watching her with hooded eyes. He indicated the Macanudo Portofino cigar he held that was gently sending tendrils of smoke curling into the air.

"I do. How are you, Stacy?" he said in his deep resonant voice, placing the thesaurus he'd been thumbing through back on its shelf.

The low vibrations of his voice flowed through her and she struggled to think of an answer. Even across the room she could feel his attraction pulling at her. She was dismayed to find its strength hadn't lessened with time; it felt as if they'd been separated for minutes instead of years.

"Fine, Ward. You're looking well," she finally answered. She hoped her commonplace words hid the enormous understatement of her last sentence. At thirty-two he looked even better than he had five years before. The potential she'd seen in him then had obviously been realized, and if he'd been attractive then, he was devastating now. Forcing her eyes away from the pull of his shirt over his muscular chest, she looked around the room.

"Where's Robbie?" she finally asked. Her motorcycle helmet swung on her fingertips as she watched him lean against the desk, the firm jaw and smooth angles of his face telling her nothing.

"In the production room. I told him we were old friends and wanted to renew our friendship in private. He agreed and offered his office."

"Why did you have to tell Robbie about us at all?" Stacy asked, her anger making her words sharp. "There was no need to dredge up the past—it has no bearing on today." She watched him as he uncrossed his legs and straightened. Why did he have to wear such close-fitting jeans?

"It has a great deal of bearing," he told her. "We're going to be working together and I don't want our . . . relationship to interfere in the newsroom."

"Interfere? How can something interfere when it doesn't exist?" Stacy asked, her disgust clearly evident in her voice. "Our 'relationship' ended five years ago."

"Ended? Or was it only interrupted?" he asked, taking a long, contemplative draw on his cigar.

"What are you talking about? Of course it ended! I married Don . . ." Stacy could have kicked herself for mentioning her late husband; Ward had not accepted her marrying Kemble with anything approaching equanimity.

At her words, Ward's eyes darkened and he ran an agitated hand through his almost black hair, the controlled waves becoming uncontrolled curls as soon as his hand passed through them. A few tumbled unnoticed onto his forehead.

"Kemble! You were a fool to marry him," he said roughly, not bothering to hide his disgust and another complex emotion Stacy didn't want to analyze. "Marrying him was the only really stupid thing I've ever known you to do."

Since she could hardly tell him how much she agreed with him, she waved her hand to dismiss the entire subject. "This is ridiculous, Ward. Too much has happened for us to go back and rehash the past."

Walking toward Roberts's desk, she threw her helmet on one of the green vinyl chairs but remained standing. She shook her head. If this conflict between them couldn't be resolved, she knew both their jobs would be unbearable. But what could she do? Thinking of offering an olive branch, she opened her mouth to speak, but his look forestalled her.

A dark, finely etched eyebrow went up as his eyes went to her helmet. "Do I detect Kemble's influence? I hope you haven't picked up any more of his habits. He had a number of bad ones, such as writing fiction and presenting it as fact."

So much for the olive branch. Frowning, she said coldly, "Don't worry, I don't invent quotes—or the people to say them." She picked up an ashtray on Roberts's desk, hoping to give her hands something to do other than strangling Ward. "I wrote good, tight, accurate copy when we worked on all those stories together at the *Beacon*—and I still do."

She was shaking with reaction. Could he really think such a thing of her? Trying to steady herself, she put the ashtray back and started to sit down when Ward's touch on her shoulder stopped her.

"That was uncalled for. I'm sorry."

The searing heat at her shoulder brought back her body's memories of his touch, the need for him that she had buried so long ago rising up to almost overwhelm her. A seductive warmth dissipated the chill his earlier words had caused, and she instinctively turned toward him. He stood so close her quick breath made the open collar of his shirt flutter as she absorbed his nearness. She tilted her head up to be face-to-face with him.

"I underst—"

His hand hovered over her right cheek in a phantom caress and his head began to lower. She was dizzy with the memory of all the pleasure his lips had given her and instead of moving out of his emotional embrace, she held her breath in anticipation of his kiss.

But Ward's head stopped a heartbeat before someone began pounding on the office door.

18

"Mr. Fallbrook! Mr. Fallbrook!" came Margaret's voice through the wood of the door. "Mr. Roberts would like to see you in Production!"

His half-closed eyes widened and he shook himself almost imperceptibly. Stacy backed away, not sure if he had actually stopped the kiss before Margaret's interruption or not. She could only be glad, whatever the reason. Gripping the back of the chair, she told herself firmly that she hadn't backed away only out of curiosity. They certainly were not going to pick up where they'd left off!

But before she could assure him of that, a distant expression fell across his features. It was not an expression she remembered seeing on his face before, and she was inexplicably saddened that it was directed toward her.

"Things have changed, haven't they, Mrs. Kemble?" he said cryptically as he walked toward the door. His hand was on the knob when he turned to her to add, "God knows why you chose the path you did. I don't." The door slammed behind him.

His last two words were spoken with such a ragged bitterness that Stacy didn't immediately follow him out into the newsroom. She still hadn't completely regained her composure when another, softer knock came on the door.

"Tell me to go away and I will," Elspeth Fremont said, peeking through the slightly open doorway. The *Monitor*'s family editor was a woman in her mid-fifties whose figure had lost none of its trimness to the years and whose aristocratic face showed few signs of aging. Only her dark hair, liberally streaked with white, gave any clue to her age.

Stacy smiled and shook her head, "Nonsense, Elly. I was just coming out."

19

"Yarrow's called—again. He says you'll be sorry if you don't talk with him," the older woman said. Grinning at Stacy's groan as the young woman rolled her eyes to the ceiling in exasperation, Elly added, "Let's hope this 'scoop' isn't as big a deadend as his last one."

"I'd better go talk to him. He's the legal counselor for most of the companies around here. One day he might actually let something drop."

"And they call *me* optimistic!" Elly laughed.

At her desk, Stacy flipped through her address book to the Ys. A frown marred her lips as she thought of the tall gangly man who was legal counselor to at least half the companies in the area surrounding Hannah. And since those companies all had something to do with agriculture, as did practically everything—and everyone—else in the San Joaquin Valley, she had to keep on top of any story that might break. Which meant keeping Yarrow as a contact, even though he was an inveterate flirt who never failed to make her want to run to the nearest shower to get clean again.

After punching the number, a new voice answered his extension. Had he had to get another secretary so soon? She explained her call and was told to wait a moment.

Yarrow came on the line with his usual attempt to draw her into a personal conversation. She ruthlessly walked over his words and reminded him of his call to her.

Putting the phone down after her conversation, she shuddered and thought wistfully of her vacation. But that didn't alter the fact that she'd had to agree to have lunch with Yarrow. The hints he'd dropped about Campbell Chemical had been too intriguing to ignore—and naturally he couldn't tell her over the phone and save her a trip and an unpleasant lunch.

20

Her eyes glanced around the newsroom of their own accord, not knowing what they were seeking until they rested on Ward's tall frame casually sitting on the edge of Elly's desk. She was furious at herself when he glanced up at that moment and, catching her eyes on him, gave a slight nod in her direction. Trying hard to look nonchalant, she let her eyes continue their circuit of the room. Her brows lowered in a frown as she realized that several other women were also casually glancing his way.

Turning back to her desk, she chastized herself for wasting time—she certainly had more important things to do.

She made a few more phone calls before signing on to her computer terminal. After scanning the summaries of the major wire stories, she started writing her own article, willing herself not to think of anything but her story. She had a good angle and her lead-in had all the punch she could want.

A half-hour later, she filed it and wrote a couple of short pieces and a sidebar to the major story. It was nearing deadline when Robbie called out to her to ask if she'd finished.

"Last one's filed right . . . now," she called, waiting for the bright-green rectangle to appear in the upper left corner of her screen, which indicated the file had been saved. She made a couple more notes—ideas that had occurred to her as she'd been writing the other stories—then wandered back to Robbie's desk.

She casually glanced at the front page layout he'd been working on, trying to see where he'd put her story but most of the page was still unmarked. As usual, he was editing her story on his screen and asking questions as he went along. Finished, he hit a key and immediately the story, which had taken up the width of the computer terminal screen, was a narrow band of words on the left side of the screen. A line at the top appeared to tell him how long the story would be when it came out of the composer.

"Twenty-four inches. Good, just what I needed," Robbie said, turning back to his front-page layout and marking the lower-left corner with a broad slash. Robbie turned back to his terminal to write the headline, which meant she was done for that day's paper.

Stacy grinned to herself as she went back to her desk. Sometimes she was sure the *Monitor*'s motto was "All the news that fits!"

She went back to her desk and began working on a story for the next day's paper. An hour later she threw the telephone receiver into its cradle in disgust. Another lead hadn't panned out and now the clock on the far wall read ten after twelve, which meant it was really about five till noon and her frown deepened. Not only could she not get any solid leads on this story of Yarrow's, but now she was going to have to face the man himself. Sighing, she knew there was nothing she could do about it but forge ahead; good reporters couldn't be fainthearted.

She retrieved her purse from the bottom drawer but before she could leave, Ward appeared at her side from nowhere, his distinctive masculine scent announcing his presence as effectively as a shout.

"I came to take you to lunch," he said. His earlier withdrawn look had been replaced by an odd speculative light in his eyes and Stacy was caught off-guard by the change. What did it mean?

She opened her mouth to decline, not wanting to explain her appointment with Yarrow, but Ward's arm had found its way around her waist and he was escorting her out of the newsroom before she had a chance to say anything. After a quick glance around the newsroom told her most of the other reporters had left, she was thankful that so few would witness his commandeering of her.

His touch left her breathless but as they neared his Saab she forced herself to say, "Ward, I can't go to lunch with you. I've got to meet Frank Yarrow."

A dark look fell across his face and the light faded in his eyes. "Who's this Yarrow?" he demanded. His hand tightened on her waist, inadvertently pulling her closer to him in his agitation. The feel of his lithe length pressed into her side mesmerized her senses and she had to force her brain to work to answer him.

"Yarrow's one of Hannah's hot-shot attorneys. He's retained by at least half the big companies in the area, so I can't very well stand him up!"

The ominous light in his eyes dimmed as he said, "I can see that. Where do we meet him?"

Stacy opened her mouth to protest, but instead she found herself telling him the name of the restaurant where she was to meet the unsuspecting lawyer.

Yarrow's thin face registered his pique at finding he was not to have Stacy to himself at lunch. At his look, Stacy had a sinking feeling that the information so profusely promised over the phone that morning was going to be a long time coming. And, to top it off, Ward gestured for her to slide into the half-circle corner booth before him—putting her between him and Yarrow; Ward's wicked grin told her he was well aware of her predicament.

"You didn't tell me you were going to bring someone along, Stacy," Yarrow said. He frowned as his pale blue eyes traveled to Ward. "I would have preferred our, er, discussion to be in private."

23

"I persuaded Mrs. Kemble to let me accompany her," Ward said.

"I thought you'd welcome the opportunity to meet the *Monitor*'s new editor, Floyd," Stacy added quickly when she saw Ward wasn't going to say anything more. She hoped she didn't sound as flustered as she thought she did, but the look on Ward's face told her she hoped in vain. Why was she acting like this? She normally handled reluctant contacts with ease. Plunging on, she said, "Ward Fallbrook takes over when Rob Roberts retires at the end of the month."

It was one of the worst meals—breakfast, lunch, or dinner—she'd ever lived through. On one side of her, Yarrow repeatedly avoided answering her questions, and insisted on sitting much too close to her. On her other side, Ward sat through the entire meal without once touching her and yet she was more aware of his presence than she would have been of a thousand Yarrows.

More than once during the meal she caught herself gazing at Ward's strong, fine-boned hands as he grasped his wineglass or unobtrusively signaled the waitress for another liter of Chablis when Yarrow's insatiable thirst threatened to make them run out.

When she'd brushed away the lawyer's hand from her leg for the third time, the unwanted image of Ward's hand when it had been there long ago flashed through her mind.

Startled by the intensity of her reaction to the memory, her green-gold gaze unconsciously flew to Ward's face to find him watching her with a faint smile playing around his lips. Surely he couldn't know what was in her mind!

To still her erratic pulse, she let visions of the calm, isolated sand dunes in Death Valley pass through her mind. She tried to imagine she was already there on her upcoming vacation, instead of grinding her teeth in frustration in a second-rate restaurant.

"I'm sorry you aren't able to tell me anything more, Floyd. Over the phone you'd said you had enough information to show Campbell's responsibility in this thing, and now . . ." Stacy let her voice trail off as the waitress cleared away their dessert plates.

Yarrow looked uncomfortable. Once the waitress had gone, he said, "A man in my position can't take too many chances." His large-knuckled hands folded his napkin into a neat, tiny square as he added, "And it's difficult to know what's important and what isn't—something that looked vital in the morning might look quite ordinary by lunchtime, you know."

No, she didn't know, Stacy wanted to scream. But she just nodded sympathetically as she planned her vengeance for Ward Fallbrook—she might have had a scoop by now if he hadn't insisted on coming along.

"I'll call you tomorrow if I can get any more information for you—don't know that I can, you understand—but I have a meeting this afternoon with Campbell and I might, just might, be able to get something for you." Yarrow looked at her with a look that told her clearly that he was doing this as a personal favor.

Irrationally blaming Ward for her own inability to keep the luncheon on a businesslike footing, she started to rack up his score and as her temper equaled the rising tally, she battled to keep her anger from overflowing her control until they were outside the restaurant.

Her high-heeled boots made a rough staccato noise on the concrete sidewalk as her anger manifested itself in her quick stride. Unfortunately her temper proved too strong and, as her steps accented each word, she said, "Do you

25

realize I'm walking out of there without a scrap more information than when I arrived! Why did you have to come along? This isn't the *Beacon* anymore; we're not reporters scooping a story together. This is *my* beat, and mine alone—and it stays that way!"

Suddenly she felt her elbow gripped in an iron grasp and started to struggle to free herself before realizing the futility of it.

Ward's eyes narrowed as he led her to his car. "You know damn good and well what Yarrow wants—and it isn't to give you a scoop for the *Monitor!*"

He unlocked the passenger door for her, then marched over to the driver's side. After jabbing the key into the ignition between the seats, he draped his arms over the steering wheel without starting the car.

Staring at the dirty stucco wall of the restaurant, Stacy said, "Damn it, Ward! I'm twenty-eight years old! And I've successfully fought off one or two lechers in my time."

His gaze pierced her and she lowered her eyes and leaned back in the seat. "No. No, you know I don't mean you." Sighing, she looked out the side window and said nothing more as she tried to convince herself that it was the situation that was rocky, not their professional relationship—they *would* be able to work together. They had to!

"Why didn't you tell me this morning Kemble had been killed?" he asked quietly, all traces of his anger gone.

She glanced at him, her eyes the color of murky jasper. Looking back out the windshield, she said, "He died over three years ago. It didn't occur to me you wouldn't know." How she hated to be reminded of Don and her years with him.

Rubbing her forehead, she said much more coldly than

26

she meant to, "Can we get back to the newsroom? I've got a lot of calls to make."

The look on his face had begun to soften as he'd watched her, but at her words it became the cool mask she'd seen earlier in Robbie's office. He reached down to turn on the ignition and she turned away again, telling herself she had to keep the distance between them—it was the only way they would be able to work together.

CHAPTER TWO

Braking to a stop at a light, the bike tilted slightly beneath her as Stacy put her weight on one foot. The dark visor of her helmet distorted her view near the edge where it curved to fit snugly against the protective material of the helmet itself, causing Mr. Johnson's drugstore to ripple on her right.

Stacy was thinking of her last interview—a man running for the recently vacated county supervisor's seat—when a tiny beep from behind her made her look guiltily at the now green light.

Turning the right handgrip toward her with a slow, smooth motion, she simultaneously released the clutch lever with her left hand and accelerated. The wind tugged lightly at her clothes as she sped along, farther and farther from the newsroom at the *Monitor* and Ward Fallbrook.

Fortunately the publisher had scheduled a meeting that afternoon between the new editor and the retiring one, so Ward had been closeted with Meeves and Robbie the rest of the day. Stacy had been able to get some excellent notes for a couple of stories she was going to do tomorrow, and she smiled as she realized that night was going to be her first free evening in a week, since the usual city council meeting had been postponed.

The traffic was light and she arrived home quickly. She went through the kitchen and slowly climbed the stairs to her bedroom, casually hanging her helmet on the doorknob and throwing her purse and portfolio on the bed as she entered her room.

After shrugging out of the clothes she'd worn all day, she donned a pair of old jeans and tied the long ends of her white shirt up under her breasts, exposing her slender waist. The poor old shirt bore signs of having had extensive exposure to her darkroom chemicals—she could never get those fix stains out.

Pulling out a file of negatives she'd planned on printing that night, she sat down at her desk and started looking through them. But after the third frame she realized she wasn't seeing the tiny pictures. Straightening, she carefully wrapped her loupe back up in its felt bag and moved the file folder to one side.

Obviously, working with Ward was going to be harder than she'd imagined. She recalled the meeting in Robbie's office that morning—had Ward really not known Don was dead? If not, Elly must have told him later that morning, which would explain the considering look she'd caught in his eyes several times during lunch. But what was he considering? The image of his head bent close to hers abruptly filled her mind and she shook her head violently to dispel it.

No! What had been between them was over. Finished. And if he didn't know it yet, he would soon get the message.

Intensity was what she remembered most about Ward and their relationship. Each time they'd be together, she'd lose a bit more of herself to him until she'd begun to fear that she would lose herself completely, just as her mother had.

And the stronger the bonds between them had been forged, the more he'd pressed for a commitment, and the more she'd desperately resisted. He didn't realize that that last surrender of herself was more than her terrified soul could do.

So, what had she done? Seeking a permanent escape from that fear, she'd accepted Don Kemble's proposal.

Bitter regret at her stupidity gripped her now. What had her arguments been? She would be safe with Don—she didn't, couldn't, love him, so she didn't walk in fear of losing herself in him. But marriage had given him a power over her she hadn't foreseen, and she shuddered at the remembered pain. Now a commitment of any kind was something she avoided, allowing herself only the most innocuous kind of relationships.

Her parents' marriage had been an unpleasant and painful thing to watch. She'd had to sit by and see her mother drowning herself in her husband while Stacy knew her father had desperately wanted someone who would stand beside him, not cower behind him.

Each parent would talk to their bright daughter as if she'd been a friend instead of their child, and they'd constantly reiterated that the other had been so very different before their marriage. It was no wonder that to the sensitive child observing them, it had seemed that marriage itself had caused their unhappiness.

She leaned back in her chair and rested her knees on the edge of the desk as she stared unseeing at the large framed print of the Kelso dunes that hung above her desk. One of the smaller prints that bristled out the sides of the frame fell down and landed in front of her. Idly, she picked it up and her heart thudded to a halt.

It was a picture she'd taken of Ward back at the *Beacon;* she'd just begun to be interested in photography and she'd finally cajoled him into posing for her. He was sitting on a bench in the little park that had been next to the newspaper's office—his legs were spread wide and his left hand was on one knee while his right elbow rested on the other and his chin rested in his hand. It wasn't the pose that had prompted her to keep the picture, however, but the expression in his eyes.

And now that warm mixture of amusement, affection, keen intelligence, and maybe a tiny dollop of desire stared out at her from the past. But she closed her eyes to the man in the picture and threw it in the trash.

Rummaging through the stack of proof sheets, negatives, and notes she had piled up after her last stint in the darkroom, she gathered a pile of them up, along with a couple of felt-tip pens and a pencil, and started to go back downstairs.

But she stopped halfway down the stairs and ran back to her room to rescue the picture. Shells from pistachio nuts rattled in the bottom of the wastebasket when she violently picked up the metal can to retrieve the portrait. As she jammed it back in place behind the large frame, she adamantly refused to think about what she was doing or why.

Finally reaching the kitchen, she plopped the proof sheets down on the table and set to work getting her dinner. Homemade beef broth went into a large kettle along with chopped-up vegetables and some leftover roast-beef. After adding the required herbs and spices, she set the timer for an hour.

31

Sitting down at the table, she began transferring her notes on exposure and development times to the backs of the proof sheets; it was tedious work, but it had to be done or she would never know how to print the shot right when she needed to.

"Ahh!" she cried, jumping in her seat as the doorbell rang and the timer went off at the same time. Laughing at her reaction, she got up and, shouting "Just a minute!" to whoever was at the door, went to turn off the burner.

Going to the door, she could see a man's vague outline through the sheer curtains over the window in the door. Her hand froze on the doorknob as she recognized who was standing there.

"We could spend the evening like this," Ward said to her through the closed door, "but it's a little difficult to squeeze roses through the mail slot."

"Ward!" She opened the door as she blurted out, "Why on earth would you get me roses?"

He chuckled and handed her the bouquet of white flowers. Leaning forward, he whispered, "I promise not to answer that if you invite me in," and before she knew what he was doing, his mouth had descended on hers.

Her lips parted in surprise as his mouth covered hers in a slow gentle kiss that made her blood course through her with a familiar languid heat. Her arms naturally started to go to his shoulders, but she stopped herself.

Breaking away, she stood back a step and looked up at him, her hands planted firmly on her hips. "One more stunt like that and you can turn around and use the nearest exit immediately! I won't let you maul me." But she couldn't deny the warmth his kiss had caused and her harsh words had no emotion behind them.

Her eyes were drawn to his sensuous lips as he grinned. "It was only a hello peck between friends."

"A peck! You call that a peck?"

"You call that getting mauled?"

Stacy had never been able to resist that teasing sparkle in his silver eyes and, to her inner disgust, she felt her lips tilt up in a smile. "Okay, *pax*. But we do have to talk about it."

"The kiss?"

"Our relationship," she said with a warning darkening her eyes. "Or rather the lack thereof."

He grinned again and nodded briefly, then sniffed the air. "That smells delicious!"

She smiled again. "That's dinner. The timer went off just as you came to the door."

"I *am* starving," he hinted, "but I suppose it's one of those individual-serving boiling bags."

"You can't smell something in plastic and you know it! Don't you need to get out and mingle with the Hannah elite? You won't meet many VIPs in my kitchen."

"Plenty of time for that later," he said, and closed his eyes as he sniffed the air again. "Actually, I just came from a cocktail party where I met half this town's bankers, lawyers, *sans* Yarrow, and wealthy proprietors. So I've done my duty, ma'am."

"Isn't seven a little early to leave?" Stacy asked.

Ward grimaced as he said, "You wouldn't ask that if you'd seen the pathetic little dried crusts of bread some heartless soul had presented as hors d'oeuvres. The spread's distinctive blue cast lacked visual appeal somehow."

"All right, all right!" she laughed. "I'll give in this time, but don't get any ideas that I'm easily maneuvered!"

"Easily maneuvered? We are talking about Tenacious Stace who used to work at the *Beacon,* aren't we?"

Giving him a look that told him what she thought of his humor, Stacy headed for the kitchen but stopped and turned to ask him a question. But it died on her lips as she watched him take off his suit jacket and throw it across the banister, his tie quickly following.

After unbuttoning three of his shirt's buttons and rolling up his sleeves, he rippled his shoulders to get comfortable and said, "There!" in a satisfied voice. The movement of his muscles under the smooth material was hypnotizing and she had to shake herself before she could turn back toward the kitchen, her question forgotten.

Once there, she had to stand and get her breath for a minute. Too bad she hadn't worked in her darkroom tonight, or she could have blamed her lightheadedness on inhaling too many chemical fumes. Ward entered and she gave him a quick smile before turning back to the sink where she gently laid the roses. She started to drag out the step stool, but he intervened.

"Do you need something you can't reach? I'll get it for you."

"Thanks, but I can manage," she answered, and, pulling the clattering metal stool in front of the corner cabinet, opened the top cupboard door and stepped up on the stool. She saw the crystal vase she was after glitter at her from the top shelf, just out of her reach. God only knew how she'd gotten it up there in the first place. With a disgusted sigh, her arm came down and she turned to Ward.

"Yes, I do need your help. Could you get that vase on the top shelf?"

"No problem," he said and reached up, putting his

hands high around her bare waist, his thumbs resting just below her unconfined breasts.

"Ward!" she cried, then found herself being lifted off the stool and onto the floor. His hands lingered there, feeling the soft silk of her skin, an odd smoky light in his eyes. "Ward," she warned.

He smiled as he put her from him, his lips grazing her forehead as he did so, and stepped up on the stool. Grasping the vase, he carefully set it down on the counter. "There you go."

Smiling her thanks, she turned to the sink and rinsed the vase out before filling it with the flowers.

Pushing her negatives and proof sheets to one side, she put the vase on the farthest corner of the table so there would be enough room to eat. She leaned over to put the finishing touches on the arrangement and when she straightened, felt his warm lips caressing the back of her neck. A shiver traveled down her spine as his kisses traced an imaginary line around the base of her neck. His hands clasped her waist and slowly drew her back against the hard muscles of his chest.

Her blood lit with a fire that blazed through her with devastating intensity. She felt herself melting against him and stiffened in surprise. "Damn it, Ward! Stop it!" she said as evenly as she could manage. "Either let me clear off the table or leave."

His teeth took one last tug on her earlobe before he released her and she ignored the sensual flame that licked up inside of her.

"You don't really expect me to sit here and watch you do all the work, do you?" he asked.

She turned around, breaking his hold on her, and saw his eyes lighten from dark silver to their usual sparkling gray. Feeling that he had accepted her rules, for the moment at least, she controlled her temper. "Why don't you clear and set the table while I finish getting dinner ready."

She couldn't prevent her eyes from returning his smile. "The dishes are in that cupboard," she said, slipping from in front of him, "and the silverware's in there."

After a pleasant dinner, during which they stayed on safe topics and discussed Ward's plans for the *Monitor,* Stacy led him into the front room, sighing over the second-hand early American furniture Don had insisted they buy. But she couldn't afford anything better now, so she motioned Ward to the sofa as she halted by a large chair covered in a faded plaid.

Warm hands clasped her shoulders and she quickly found herself looking up into dark, silver eyes. His mouth began to descend to hers, but she ignored the roaring in her veins with a sigh of exasperation. So much for her threats to throw him out.

Hearing her sigh, his lips teased the corners of her mouth with tiny, devastating kisses instead of the full kiss she had expected.

"You don't give up, do you?" she asked, frowning at the words, which came out much less stern than she'd wanted them to. "Ward, we've got to talk."

"Do we? Why? There are so many other—" Her lips tightened into a thin line and he stopped. Giving a barely audible sigh, he raised his head and said, "All right, Stacy, we'll talk."

He sat down beside her on the faded red and blue plaid sofa and put his arm along the back of it. The nerves along her shoulders were intensely aware of his arm only inches from her, and when his fingers lightly brushed her hair,

her and her body jerked at the strength of it. His hands pulled her closer into his embrace.

He explored the smooth caverns and tiny ridges of her mouth, leaving no part of it undiscovered to his questing tongue and leaving no part of her mouth unfired by that darting, devastating flame.

One hand caressed her neck and his fingers journeyed into the glowing mane of her long hair until they could resist no longer, and they twined themselves around the dark fiery strands.

His other hand was rhythmically smoothing the silken skin of her bare back, the lengthening strokes taking him farther and farther up under her blouse to her shoulders. Only distantly did she feel his hand high on her side until it found its way to her breast and his fingers began to tease the very end of her tautened nipple. Her body stiffened at the sensations flashing through her like an internal meteor shower sending long tails of burning light through her veins.

How could his touch still wind her up to such an aching tightness? She leaned into the smooth hard muscles of his body, as if to find the source of his power and unleash the energy now so tightly caught within her. The soft flesh of her thighs melted against his hard, muscled legs and she knew a sudden desire to know all of him, to feel all of the movements of his body under her hands.

Only vaguely realizing what she was doing, her arms slid from around his neck and started to undo the rest of the buttons on his shirt. A sigh ran through her at the electric touch of the hardness of his flesh beneath the of dark curls covering his chest.

His lips left her mouth and trailed tiny kisses along her jaw to her ear, there to further devastate her senses. Her head bent back and the green-gold eyes closed to savor the sensual chills his nibbling teeth sent down her spine. The old familiar maelstrom began to brew inside her, pulling at the very sense of her being and drawing her down into its seductive, mindless pool of sensation.

"Could Don ever make you feel like this?" he murmured against her ear.

Stacy's senses went cold as his words jolted her back to the present. She felt Ward's muscles tense at her reaction and she stepped back from his embrace.

He straightened and looked at her with regret in his eyes before he took a deep breath and absently tugged his shirt back into place, but left it unbuttoned.

"Stacy . . ."

With his hair an uncontrolled mass of curls spilling over onto his forehead, his eyes still dark with desire, and his shirt open almost to his waist, revealing the hard chest under the dark hair, he made her catch her breath at her own desire for him. No! She wouldn't allow herself to respond to him, though she had to fight the emotion that stabbed through her at the sight he made.

Angry at her own desire, she cried, "No apologies! Just leave me, Ward, just leave me alone." Her eyes were shooting golden sparks as she spat out her words.

"Why do you fight what's between us?" he asked. "We've always belonged together." His hands reached up to grasp her shoulders, but she wrenched away. His eyes narrowed at her action and his voice was a low, even-toned threat as he added, "And I'm not going to let you slip away again."

"Well, you're definitely going to have to live without me for the next week. I'm leaving for Death Valley tomorrow

40

night but when I get back I will make you understand that I do not belong to you or anyone else."

She started to storm out of the room when she turned back to him, her mouth opening to say something, but all that came out was, "And button up your damn shirt!"

"Stacy!" Ward called after her as she ran toward the stairs, slamming the bedroom door behind her.

Her motorcycle helmet rocked back and forth on the doorknob. She reached out to stop it, but her hand closed around the chin strap instead. Before she fully realized what she was doing, it was on her head and, after grabbing a jacket, she was running back down the stairs and out to the garage to her bike.

The garage door opened and she silently backed it out into the street, not really caring if she made a great deal of noise or not.

Once there, she saw a vague figure through the window in her front door and realized Ward was waiting for her to return. She fired up the bike and sped off down the street; he was going to have a long wait.

In her turmoil she didn't see the tall, slender form that ran out to the curb to watch her go.

For the first few minutes she thought of nothing but leaving the small town behind. When she finally passed the abandoned gas station that marked the town line, she jerked the throttle forward and flew along the old country road, letting the wind batter the anger from her body.

It was madness for him not to believe her! She lost count of the dark, silent farmhouses she passed as her arguments ran through her mind. She had to make Ward understand.

Suddenly a sharp corner appeared ahead and she just had time to brake lightly as she put out her left foot and tilted the bike around in a controlled skid. Seconds later she slowed the bike to a halt and parked it on the side of the road under a large stand of live oaks.

She swung her leg over the seat and got off the bike. Moving carefully because her legs and arms were shaking with the adrenaline that had shot through her, Stacy sat down in a tree's faint shadow cast by light of the half-moon and took deep breaths.

What a fool she was being! Running away from him again wouldn't solve her problem, and she knew better than to try to ride her motorcycle when she was upset.

Calm started to return and her eyes idly scanned the eerie night landscape; the light from the half moon gave a gray luminescent quality to the fields. She remembered Ward's eyes were that same color gray when they were filled with laughter, then she brusquely pushed that thought away.

The squeal of tires interrupted her and she turned to face the corner just in time to have a car's headlights blind her. It was a good indication of her state of mind that she felt no fear when the car came to an abrupt halt, the dirt and rocks on the side of the road protesting the violent braking.

But her unease grew when the driver got out of the car and started walking toward her, the crunch of gravel under his feet adding a steady beat to the otherwise still night.

Her hand had belatedly started searching out something to use as a weapon when the scent of a cigar reached her. She tensed now for a different reason as she watched the glowing red end come nearer. His voice cut across the night.

"Stacy! Are you all right?"

"I'm fine, Ward," she called to him in an even voice.

The crunching of the gravel stopped as he halted in front of her. Her head bent back as her eyes slowly traveled up to his face; it was difficult to see his expression in the moonlight, but she knew he wasn't smiling.

He sat down beside her on the clump of grass and she felt his slight trembling. The corner must have caught him by surprise too. "Running away again?" he mocked.

When she said nothing, he continued. "Okay, Stacy, I won't give in, but I'll play it your way for a while."

Her elbows were resting on her drawn-up knees and she sighed and hung her head between them. "It's not a game, Ward. It's my life, and I don't want you in it."

She heard him exhale slowly, the smell of his cigar smoke wafting passed her. Raising her head to look at him, she saw he was watching her.

Folding her legs under her, she turned slightly to face him. "How can I make you believe me? I've spent all evening trying to convince you! You've got to be the most bullheaded—" She stopped and shook her head; that would get her nowhere. "I made one wrong, very wrong, commitment in my life, and I don't plan on making another one."

"It wouldn't've been wrong with me."

"You don't know that! I was twenty-three when we had our . . . affair and I'm a different person now than I was five years ago. The Stacy Peterson you knew doesn't exist anymore; you don't know Stacy Kemble at all."

"I'm not going to let an ass like Don Kemble keep you from me, Stacy. Whatever your relationship with him was or wasn't—it's over. I want you and I'll get you."

She got to her feet and stood before him with fists on her hips. "You can't 'get' me if I don't let you, and I won't.

43

And don't you dare badger me in the newsroom because I warn you, I'll fight for my job at the *Monitor.*"

Looking up at her as if to gauge her sincerity, he took another pull on his cigar and let the smoke drift from his mouth before he answered her. "Stacy, am I battling your feelings for me or your feelings about commitments? A lifetime is a long time for you to pay for one mistake. And *I* don't intend to pay for it at all."

She was silent for a moment, digesting his words. The three years she'd spent with Don flashed through her mind; the long bitter arguments, the careless insults, and that terrible feeling of being trapped in a cage of her own making.

"Back off, Ward," she warned.

He stood up, and traced a finger down the firm edge of her jaw to her chin and in the faint light Stacy could see his lips drawn in a taut line as his eyes searched her face.

"No," he growled, "I won't let you hide."

She stepped back from his touch. "I'm not hiding from anything. I just want to be left alone; we'll see each other at the *Monitor,* but that's all, nothing else."

He threw his cigar down and violently heeled it into the ground. Grabbing her shoulders in a fierce grip, he leaned down until his face was inches from hers. "I won't let you stay away from me—I've told you that."

He relaxed his grip and added in a ragged whisper, "Let me go on seeing you and I'll stop pressing you about our relationship. You can't imagine how long these past five years have been."

Stacy took a breath to deny him, but the words stopped in her throat. It was a compromise she didn't want, but she knew it was all he would give her. Battling him was wearing her down, taking energy she didn't have in excess, and she realized with a defeated sigh that she would agree.

"All right, I'll agree to us seeing each other casually, nothing more."

"That's enough . . . for now."

The gravel rustled under his feet as he walked back to his car without giving her a chance to reply. He slammed the door and gunned the engine to a roar and, making a tight U-turn in the road, sped back to town, leaving her to watch the path of his headlights in the darkness.

Her steps were sluggish as she walked back to her bike. She couldn't forget the passion of their kiss or the desire she'd seen in his eyes as they'd broken apart. How long would he abide by their agreement?

And on the heels of the unwelcome memory of her own response came the unsettling thought: How long would she?

CHAPTER THREE

"Good story, Stacy," Robbie said, hitting the file key on his computer terminal. "How about a sidebar on other recent accidents involving large farming machinery. About fifteen inches should do it, okay?"

Stacy nodded and went back to her terminal, quickly typing out the requested story. Since she'd had to do research on that subject anyway for the main story, it didn't take much time to dig through her notes and finish the sidebar.

The reporter whose desk was in front of hers in the crowded newsroom was looking at her with a strange expression on his face, and it took her a moment to realize her humming was causing it. She grinned and stopped immediately, but not before she saw him shake his head.

Laughing to herself, she hit the file key with a flourish and sat back in her chair. Her phone calls that morning had gone well and her questions had been answered quickly and succinctly—unusual at any time—and to top it all off, Yarrow hadn't called once. Surely that was enough to explain her good mood.

She'd dreaded coming to work that morning, but now she wondered at her own reaction. How could she have been so distressed? The chair creaked when she leaned back for a moment, thinking that Ward's sudden reappearance in her life had rocked her emotions violently, as if someone had carelessly stepped into a small boat. But now she assured herself with a smile, the water was once again calm and undisturbed.

Her smile was still in place when she called to Robbie that the sidebar was done. Rustling papers told her someone was behind her, and she spun her chair around and found Ward sitting on the edge of her desk, his lips curving up in an answering smile.

"How about lunch?" he asked, not letting the lowering corners of her lips deter him.

Her blood jumped in her veins at the sight of him so near. Didn't he remember their agreement? She was about to remind him of it when she stopped; something in the way he was watching her told her he had already remembered. Her eyes followed the rhythmic swing of the long muscular leg nearest her, the dark-blue denim of his jeans stretching slightly with each movement. He was sitting close, but that could have been from necessity on the small desk.

"Lunch? Did you have someplace in mind?" she asked.

Just then Floyd Yarrow walked into the newsroom, his lips retreating from his teeth in an effective rebuttal against the adage that one should always wear a smile. The unwelcome face hovered near Ward's left shoulder and Stacy suddenly knew what a small animal feels when a trapdoor starts to close.

Without waiting for Ward to answer her question, she grabbed her purse and stood up. "I'd love to!"

Ward frowned at her sudden turnabout, but stood and lightly put his arm around her waist to escort her out of the newsroom. Turning, he stopped short at the sight of

47

Yarrow standing behind him and there was a suspicious glint in his eyes as he glanced toward Stacy.

"Oh, Mr. Yarrow!" Stacy exclaimed in her best feigned-surprise voice. "I'm so sorry I can't stay and talk, but I was just leaving for lun—an appointment with Mr. Fallbrook. Perhaps I can catch you later." She scurried out of the newsroom and breathed a sigh of relief at hearing only Ward's footsteps behind her.

"I must remember to thank him the next time I see him," Ward said, his voice an intense whisper.

The large glass doors to the lobby closed behind them as Stacy looked up at him with a puzzled frown. "Thank Yarrow! Whatever for?"

"For our lunch together," he said, opening his car's door for her. "You were all set to say no until he showed up."

Flushing at the truth of his words, she tried to deny it with a weak "No, I . . ." but the slamming of the door cut her off.

"But since you are here, I thought we'd try that coffee shop out by highway ninety-nine," he said as the Saab hummed to life immediately.

The place he'd mentioned catered to truckers—not exactly what Stacy'd had in mind, but she wasn't about to say no at that point and she nodded her agreement.

Seeing the huge diesel rigs in both the enormous parking lot and on a dirt lot across the road, Ward slowed to a crawl and gave Stacy a look of disgust. "You could've told me it was a truck stop," he said, pulling into one of the few car-sized parking spaces.

"How was I to know you didn't realize it?" Stacy asked, a touch of petulance creeping into her voice. "Everyone around here does—they'll proudly tell you it's one of the largest in the state and just as proudly hold their noses up in the air if you suggest eating here."

He reached over and put his index finger on the bridge of her nose and his thumb under the straight tip, his eyes narrowing as if measuring something critically.

"I'd say yours is about as high as it usually is—so I guess we're staying. Hope it's better than some truck stops I've been in."

The touch of his fingers on her skin had sparked a current through her nervous system and she had to concentrate to stem the unfortunate sensation. To cover her involuntary reaction, she reached for the door handle and, moving her face away from his touch, stepped out of the car. She had to squeeze between it and a gargantuan tire to make her way to the restaurant door.

They were hit by a wall of sound as they entered, the coffee shop having been built to accommodate the greatest number without a thought to acoustics. The noise generated by so many differing opinions bounced off the walls of the large room, echoing back to the ears of the room's occupants as the blaring country-western music added its own counterpoint.

"Are you sure you want to eat here?" Ward said, leaning close to Stacy's ear to make himself heard.

His breath teased the tiny hairs near her ear and a shudder rippled down her spine. She looked around the coffee shop. Truck drivers of every shape, size, and sex filled the red vinyl booths, hurriedly shoveling in their food as they threw out bits of road wisdom between mouthfuls.

But one thing reassured Stacy as her photography-trained eye traveled over the cadaverous old men, the hulking bears, the pot-bellied beer drinkers, and the various women—that wherever Floyd Yarrow had decided to have lunch, it wouldn't be here.

She nodded her answer to Ward and she made a mental note to ask Robbie about coming back to the coffee shop after her vacation to do a feature story on truck drivers with an accompanying photo essay.

The waitress sailed by at that moment, holding six plates of steaming food along her arms. The woman appeared to be in her late forties and looked harried, but that didn't prevent her eyes from slowly going over Ward. Smiling and giving Stacy a wink, she used her chin to point out an empty booth in a far corner. "There's an empty booth way down at the end. Somebody'll be with you in a minute."

Seating themselves, Stacy felt Ward's ironic gaze on her as she studiously bent over the menu, trying to read it through unidentifiable stains. Peeking over the top of the ragged paper she held, her eyes were caught by his slate gaze.

"Don't you see anything you want?" she asked. His eyes remained on her and she saw the muscles in his cheeks draw his lips back, the phantom smile barely creasing the corners of his mouth. Blushing despite her disgust, she lowered her eyes back to her own menu and said, *"From the menu,* Ward. Isn't there anything you want *from the menu.*"

Furious at his unspoken innuendo, her fingers itched to tighten around the catsup bottle and heave it at his head. But she had to be satisfied with subtler methods.

"Why don't you try the fried liver and onions?" she suggested sweetly. "I know they're your favorites."

Ward was still chuckling as the waitress arrived to take their order, but his smile faded after she left.

The darkness in his eyes told her he was going to bring up the events of last night and she frantically sought a diversion. Looking out the nearby window, she noticed an excrutiatingly thin old man nimbly climbing up into one of the rigs and recalled her earlier idea.

"What do you think Robbie would say if we did a feature about truckers when I get back? Maybe have a photo essay to accompany the main story and a couple of bio sidebars . . . why are you grinning like that? It's a good idea!"

His eyes were filled with a warm laughing light that held her captive. She could feel the corners of her mouth lift in answer, though she still didn't know what he found so amusing.

"Honey, what Robbie might or might not have to say about it won't matter in the least when you get back."

The confusion in her eyes lifted immediately. How could she have forgotten! "That was silly of me to forget Robbie's retiring; it was just habit."

"What habit, Stacy?" he asked softly, "Thinking of Roberts as your editor—or of us as a team?"

The light in his eyes told her he already knew the answer. He was right; she had easily fallen into their old patterns. Even during that tense first meeting in Robbie's office, she'd suddenly felt complete again just because of Ward's presence. It was dangerous to feel that way and she desperately wanted to deny it, but the words stuck in her throat and she remained silent as the waitress delivered their food.

He seemed to enjoy making her feel uneasy and she instinctively rebelled against the manipulation. The green glint in her eyes cooled to gold as she asked in her best reporter's voice, "So what do *you* think of a story done

51

here. It wouldn't be glamorous, and only mildly titillating, but these people pass through here probably once a week at least—and nobody knows much about them or their lives."

Cutting off a small bite of steak that was surprisingly good, she held her fork in her left hand, continental-style —with the tines down—as she carried the bite to her mouth. But her hand stopped midway as she raised her eyes to Ward's face to wait for his answer and saw him grinning at her. Instantly she turned the fork over and finished her hand's movement.

He would have to remember her trivial habits. That childhood trait that she'd picked up when living during the summer with her Grandmère Peterson only occasionally snuck out in times of stress and betrayed the state of her nerves. She fumed silently at Ward for remembering. And from the silver light in his eyes, he also remembered when he'd last teased her about it. That had been the last dinner—and night—they'd had together. She harshly suppressed her body's trembling at the memory of that sensual meal.

"The trucker story," she prompted, careful to transfer the fork from her left to right hand after she sliced off another bite.

At her tone, the silver light dimmed, making his eyes as difficult to read as mercury was to hold. Another grin flashed on his mouth, but reached no further before he turned to look at the people around him.

"It is a good idea—but I'd want a completely different angle on the story before I'd okay it," he said. "Trucker stories were really overdone during the CB craze—the new American cowboy and all of that."

"Are you saying no?"

"I'm saying research it a little more before asking me about it," he said.

The waitress came and refilled Ward's coffee cup and Stacy watched with a silent frown as he peeled the lid back from the tiny plastic cream container. Slowly stirring his coffee, he added, "At the *Beacon,* you always had some solid research behind you before you'd even think about approaching the editor on a feature."

The knife-edged words slid between her ribs to pierce her heart. Forcing herself not to gasp at the pain, she deliberately fanned her anger to maintain control.

How dare he criticize her! All she'd done was casually mention a topic over lunch and he was treating her like a greenhorn! Molten gold swallowed the emerald in her eyes as her anger mounted. A small voice tried to tell her something must be wrong—it wasn't like Ward to emphasize authority unnecessarily—but the faint words were smothered by her pain.

Thank God she was going to be gone for a week! But it was difficult to think of the quiet serenity of Death Valley through the rage that boiled in her head. The sand dunes and salt flats were only indistinct images in her mind as she grasped the picture of Ward as a newsroom tyrant. It was certainly safer to think of him that way instead of as he'd looked with silver laughter in his eyes.

"Whatever you say, Mr. Fallbrook," she said in tones so cold ice could have dripped off of each word.

"Stacy—" he began, but he was interrupted when the waitress appeared with the check. Waving away her offer of dessert, he glanced at his watch. "Damn. I've got to get back to the *Monitor* for another one of Meeves's meetings."

When Stacy started to rise, she felt his restraining hand

on her arm. "Have dinner with me tonight," he said, his words polite, but his face giving away nothing of his emotions.

She continued to rise, shaking off his hand. "Sorry, I need to pack—I'm leaving tonight about midnight." She felt a sting of satisfaction at the offhand tone of her voice. Surely he would get the message she wasn't interested!

Ward was quiet on the drive back to the *Monitor* and Stacy was grateful. Her eyes watched his hand smoothly shifting through the gears, the muscles of his left leg tensing each time he engaged the clutch. She feared her nerves would snap if she didn't get away from him. His nearness was assaulting her, making her already ragged temper in danger of shredding apart completely.

"Why are you leaving so late?" he demanded abruptly, turning onto Hannah's main street.

"On my vacation? Because of the heat," she answered sharply, her tone telling him that anyone should know the answer to his question. "I have to cross the desert to get to Death Valley and even in late October traveling during the day would be foolhardy, not to mention an engraved invitation to sunstroke."

His eyes narrowed. "What kind of car are you driving?"

"I'm not driving any kind of car—I'm riding my motorcycle."

"The hell you are!" he bellowed, slamming on the brakes, the car obeying his whim with an aloof silent acceptance. Fortunately they were at the lone traffic signal in Hannah and it was red, though Stacy had the definite impression that he'd have screeched to a halt no matter where they'd been.

"That's crazy! You can't go traveling alone—*at night yet*—on a motorcycle!" His words were bursting out of him as he continued down the street to the *Monitor*'s parking lot. "Look, I'll let you drive my TransVan. It's one of the least bulky recreational vehicles on the market. You won't have any trouble with it at all."

"I know I won't have any trouble with it since I'll be on my BMW!" Did he really think her so incapable? He was acting as if she were only recently allowed out of the house by herself!

"What do you think you are? Some kind of Night Rider, deliberately courting danger? You'll drive my van!" He pulled into the lot at the *Monitor* and yanked up on the parking brake with a harsh mechanical sound.

Stacy jumped out of the Saab, Ward quickly following suit. They glared at each other across the roof of the car, their features distorted in the curving metal surface by their anger.

"You have no right to say *anything* about my actions. I am leaving for Death Valley at midnight," she said, the door slamming shut with a solid sound. She walked a couple of paces toward the entrance and turned back to him.

"On my motorcycle . . ." She took a couple of more steps toward the door and turned again.

"Alone!" She pivoted on one foot and stalked into the building, oblivious to the stare of the receptionist.

At her desk she snatched up the few phone messages, decided which ones would keep, and asked another reporter to handle the two that wouldn't and was marching out the side door to her motorcycle before Ward had entered the building.

Once at home her anger slowly dissipated. She began packing, and the necessity of making every cubic inch

55

count in the two saddle bags and the small trunklike boot pushed everything else from her mind.

Her camera equipment went into the boot after she lined the bottom and sides with a dense gray foam. Other pieces of the thick material were snuggly tucked in between the two camera bodies, four lenses, and a motor drive. The carrying case for the camera once she got there held countless rolls of film and necessary filters and she gently stuffed it into a corner. The only thing left to do was pray the vibrations from her motorcycle didn't damage the delicate optics.

She carefully packed her clothes into the two saddle bags and then attached them to her bike. After strapping on two canteens of water with bungee cords, her tent and sleeping bag were strapped on behind her on the passenger seat. She stepped back with a satisfied sigh; she was ready. Well, almost, she amended as she looked down at the rumpled pants suit she'd worn all day.

After a warm shower she pulled on a light pair of insulated underwear and then a pair of jeans and a pale blue chamois shirt. She knew from experience that though the desert might be blistering hot during the day, the nights could be anywhere from chilly to downright freezing. The weather reports had said the day's mild temperature was expected to continue, but Stacy didn't believe in taking chances. The clouds she'd seen over the distant Sierra Nevada mountains had overridden how warm the day had been in Hannah.

By the time she'd finished a hearty supper and enveloped her slender figure in a bulky down jacket, it was eleven thirty. She'd gone over her list three times and hadn't discovered anything she'd forgotten, so deciding it was ridiculous to wait for a deadline she'd set arbitrarily anyway, she set the automatic light switches and locked up the house.

It was nearing three in the morning as she sped along the two-lane highway across the Mojave Desert. The night landscape was magical; time and the rest of the earth were suspended from her consciousness and it was easy to imagine the tall spiky forms of the Joshua trees that were scattered across the land as knights resting after a skirmish with Suleiman's heathen infidels. But only half her mind was busy with mythical battles; the other half was alert to the real surroundings as she crested one tiny hillock after another on the roller-coaster road.

Suddenly the skin on the back of her neck tightened in warning. The phantasms disappeared instantly and her eyes searched the road for danger.

Her bones felt the rumbling, though the wind pummeling her body drowned out any sound she might have heard. Quickly looking north, she scanned the sparse landscape but could see little in the faint gray light.

Was there a train somewhere she couldn't see? Her motorcycle dipped down into another, wider arroyo as she tried to figure out what was wrong. The rumble increased in intensity, as if she were nearing the source. Her eye caught an old broken Joshua tree lying next to the road and suddenly she remembered what the warning meant.

Flash flood! As soon as the words entered her mind, her stomach muscles tightened and an insect of fear scurried down her spine. Now she could recognize the evidence of previous floods all around her and, without another thought, her right hand gave the throttle a violent twist.

Tucking her knees in close to the side of the bike, she hunched over to give herself the most aerodynamic profile she could. She thought of Ward's last words to her and smiled ruefully before her consciousness forced out everything else but her goal: the high, safe mesa a quarter mile away.

She crested the mesa as the roar of the water drowned out the wind and the sound from her motorcycle, but she couldn't make her hand ease up on the throttle. Behind her, she knew, the grotesque Joshua trees, creosote bushes, and other desert plant life were being ripped up by their roots and carried ruthlessly down the canyon until the dry earth finally absorbed the alien water.

A couple of miles farther brought her to a small town and a California highway patrol barricade. She was finally able to release her grip and slow down.

"Are you all right, sir?" the California highway patrolman asked as she brought the bike to a halt in the pool of light cast by the streetlamp. Her shaky nerves combined with the humor of the situation and she felt hysterical laughter bubbling at the base of her throat. A couple of quick deep breaths brought it under nominal control, though a wide grin remained as she loosened the strap of her helmet.

She shook out her chestnut curls and the streetlight caught the firelights in her hair as she turned her smile on the patrolman. His dark blond eyebrows shot up and he whistled low, obviously pleased by his mistake.

"Pardon me, *ma'am*." She could read the speculation in his eyes as they traveled over the down jacket and she perversely left it fastened as he continued. "The road's closed ahead because of a flash flood. It'll be several hours before it's cleared, but the café's open for stranded travelers if you'd like a cup of coffee." He indicated a small nearby building with light spilling out onto square patches on the ground outside.

"That's just what I need," Stacy said, getting off her bike and rolling it to the café's parking lot. Toeing down the kickstand, she saw that the highway patrolman had accompanied her. Wondering what to say to him, she looked up at the stars twinkling in the clear night sky. "I guess that storm finally broke in the Sierra—I just missed getting caught in a flash flood myself a couple of miles back. Being covered in mud is not the way I'd envisioned spending my Friday night."

"On that bike, being covered in mud is the least that would have happened to you," he said. He motioned for her to accompany him as he walked back to his patrol car to radio to the road crews about the other flash flood.

As they approached the café, another policeman walked out of it and, after a quick glance at Stacy, nodded to her escort with a grin. "Fred, one of these days *I'm* going to be going on my break just as a gorgeous lady drives up. It's just not fair for one man to have so much luck," he said with a mock sigh before continuing on toward the police car at the barricade.

Stacy sighed as the tired waitress refilled the small metal pot with hot water for the twentieth time. The caffeine from the five cups of coffee and who knew how many cups of tea was mixing with her weariness to make her temper uneven and her stomach queasy. She should have ordered something to eat earlier, but when Fred's hamburger had arrived, her appetite had suddenly vanished.

Watching the patrolman reenter the café after another hour stint at the barricade, she braced herself for another lengthy story that would finally wind down to a dull, predictable end. The man didn't want a conversation, what he wanted was an echo chamber so the only thing he'd have to hear was his own voice.

He smiled the same wide smile she'd seen earlier as he sat down across from her at the small table, and she wondered if he slept with a coat hanger in his mouth to keep his lips stretched out. But she was instantly contrite when his next words were of road conditions instead of another story.

"The road crew just passed through saying the westbound road was clear," he said. "Eastbound was hit harder, but they should have it cleared up pretty soon."

At last! Ready to escape right then, Stacy reached down to the seat next to hers and picked up her helmet. "Thank goodness!" she said with relief. "Another minute and I was ready to pitch my tent out in the parking lot!"

She was half out of her seat when a pair of headlights of a car pulling into the café's parking lot shone directly into her eyes. Instinctively shutting them against the glare, she sat down hard on the molded orange seat to avoid the lights. When she was finally able to open them again, her eyes focused on a small recreational vehicle with bold stripes across the vanlike front parked just outside the window. Her stomach stirred uneasily.

Shaking her head to dismiss such silliness, she smiled a farewell to Fred and started to rise again when a movement at the door drew her eyes. Half-standing, she froze in place as she watched a familiar dark head scan the small café's patrons. When his gray-eyed gaze found her, she slowly sank to her chair. Why did she suddenly feel like a prize butterfly waiting for the pin?

Without waiting for an invitation, Ward scraped out the chair next to hers and sat down. He leaned toward her,

60

one arm resting along the back of her chair while the other was planted firmly in front of her. The others in the restaurant faded into a colorless backdrop for her oscillating nerves and quickened breathing.

"You're damned lucky you're not washed up in a mudbank somewhere! How *could* you take off like that!" he said, anger barely held beneath the surface of his low voice.

Stacy watched the shock and chagrin flow across the patrolman's face as he listened to Ward, his former friendliness turning to wariness. She fumed at the newsman's obvious possessiveness.

"Why did you follow me?" she demanded in an angry whisper. "Damn it—you agreed to give me some room!"

A suddenly nervous Fred cleared his throat and stood up quickly. "I'd better go check on the eastbound road," he said, and, the bright overhead light flashed in reflection on the café's door as he hastily exited.

"Your friend seemed anxious to leave," Ward said, the sarcasm in his voice barely cutting into her anger. "Did he try to save you too? You didn't used to attack people who tried to help you. Is it one of Kemble's tricks you picked up?"

"What is this? You're upset because you *didn't* find me buried in the mud, aren't you?"

"Don't be ridiculous!" he answered, leaning back in his chair, but not before she'd seen the flush creeping up his neck.

"You wanted to play the hero and now you're ticked off because I didn't cooperate!"

Ward's fist crashed down on the table top. "Damn it! Ever since I heard the police scanner in the newsroom say this road was closed because of a flash flood, I've had

61

visions of you lying somewhere covered in mud. I tear out here, breaking every speed limit on the books, follow two feet behind the road crews to be the first through the flooded area, and what do I discover when I get here? Stacy Kemble flirting with a highway patrolman!"

"Flirting! Can't you tell the difference between flirting and conversing?" Green sparks struck against the gold fury in her eyes, forcing him to follow her movements as she rose, her hand snatching her helmet and tucking it under her arm. "Think what you like. I'm going on to Death Valley."

Turning blindly, she had to stop short to keep from barreling into Fred. Glancing warily at Ward, his smile wasn't nearly so wide as he said, "The eastbound road is open now. Have a safe trip. Ma'am." He nodded his head on the last word and quickly moved on to the next table.

Giving Fred a look of disgust for his cowardice, Stacy pivoted on the ball of her right foot and started toward the door. But some demon urged her to stop and turn back to Ward, saying loudly, "You will try not to speed on your way back to Hannah, won't you?"

"Who said I'm going back to Hannah?"

Frustrated that the glass door failed to give a satisfying slam as it closed behind her, she jammed the helmet on her head, leaving the visor up. The cool early morning air felt good against her flushed face. She walked to her motorcycle, each step on the asphalt pounding the image of Ward Fallbrook further from her mind.

Her eyes scanned the horizon. It was just turning the deep turquoise of a false dawn as her hand turned the key and her left foot tapped the shifter down into first.

Heading east on her bike, Stacy concentrated on getting

through the devastated area quickly, careful to stay within the narrow boundaries on the slippery road surface.

Banks of mud had been piled on both sides by the road crew and the spiky trunks of Joshua trees stuck out at odd angles, looking as if they had been carelessly tossed aside by a bored child. But she was soon past the three branches of the arroyo and, slowing pulling forward on the throttle, began adding to the miles between her and Ward.

The dawn was real now and she could see the endless plains of sand broken by distant mountains. There were few vehicles of any kind out at that time of the morning, and she reveled in the feeling of solitude.

Here she felt she could be truly alone and begin to sort out all the questions Ward's unexpected arrival had resurrected; questions she'd thought she'd dealt with and dismissed had risen again to haunt her. Ward's presence had forced her to acknowledge that she'd just run away from answering them before.

Shaking her head to clear it of the unwanted ghosts, a tiny speck in her rearview mirror caught her eye. She'd noticed it a half-hour earlier, but her musings had pushed it out of her mind. Now it was closer and she frowned at the distinctive shape of an overly large van. Surely he hadn't meant it when he'd said he would follow her—he was needed back at the *Monitor!* But as she downshifted the BMW to take a sharp turn, the bright, bold stripes stood out against the white vehicle as the van closed the gap between them.

She'd obviously been wrong not to take his threat to follow her seriously. A brown sign dulled by blasting sand told her the turnoff for Death Valley was a half-mile ahead. Sighing, she turned and couldn't prevent her eyes

63

from checking the mirror. The TransVan had turned as well.

Damn him! Instead of a week of relaxation and photography, she was now going to have to spend her time dealing with him, making him understand that—once and for all—any relationship between them was in the past!

The corners of her lips dipped further in a frown as she remembered her unconscious reaction when he had entered the small café. She shook her head, trying to deny the welcome relief that had momentarily tightened her chest, as she passed a signpost marking the distance to Furnace Creek.

Unfortunately there was no signpost to tell her how far she would have to go before she had reached that other, more distant destination where she would finally convince Ward Fallbrook that their relationship couldn't be picked up where they'd left off. But even as she glanced again at the image in the mirror, she wondered what would happen when they finally reached the campground.

She caught her breath at the surge of anticipation that shot through her and her left hand curled into a fist of frustration. Damn him again! Now she roundly cursed that astuteness of his that she'd so often praised in the past, knowing he would see her doubts. How could she hope to convince him when her own heart wasn't convinced?

CHAPTER FOUR

The sunlight was playing over the peaks of the Panamint Range as Stacy pulled into the campground. Winding around the trail to a campsite in the farthest corner, she ignored the blue-striped vehicle that seemed to be a permanent image in her rearview mirror.

Weary from the night's events, she pulled into the parking spot next to a stone picnic bench and, not looking at the TransVan pulling into the site next to hers, began to unload a minimum of gear.

She threw the ground cover on the flattest area, and was kneeling down to pound the stakes into the dirt when she heard the engine on the van cut off and a door open and close.

Her body tensed, but he remained silent and, without looking up, she continued to position the aluminum stake.

"I hope you're finding your trip amusing," she said. When that stake was finished, she was forced to go to the opposite corner of the gray plastic sheet.

She was facing him now, and not to look up would have been childish. He was leaning against the end of the stone table, his legs and arms crossed in front of him. His face was impassive as he watched her, and she couldn't tell his mood at all. Not that it mattered. Whacking the stake soundly she added, "Because I'm not."

"Why does my being here upset you so?" he asked, his question coming just as she was pulling out the third corner of the ground cover.

Startled by his response and surprised at his question, she pulled harder on it than she'd meant to, causing the plastic to tear around the grommet in the corner she was holding.

"Damn," she muttered. She'd meant the curse for Ward as much as the torn plastic.

"Look, Ward," she said finally, the dull ringing from pounding the stakes punctuating her words. "I've been planning this trip for over a year. It's one of my favorite photographic areas and I won't have you ruining it for me!"

On the last word she missed the stake on the downswing and hit the dirt. She looked at the inch-deep hole in the ground in exasperation.

"You don't have to be doing this—there's an extra bed in the van," Ward said, taking the hammer and fourth stake from her and finishing securing the ground cover.

Giving him a look that was sufficient answer to his offer, she undid the tent. It went up quickly, Stacy accepting Ward's help with a few terse instructions.

Throwing the tiny roll of her mattress pad into the tent along with her sleeping bag, she said, "Thanks for your help. I'm going to sack out for a few hours."

She started to add that she'd see him later, but closed her mouth with a snap, afraid he would take the pleasantry as acceptance of their situation—which she most certainly did not! Unlatching the boot from the back of her motorcycle, she set it in one corner of the small tent and

66

ostentatiously zipped up the tent's opening, leaving Ward standing outside with his brows lowered in a frown.

It was hot! Waking in the late morning to the sound of pacing footsteps outside her tent, Stacy reached up and unzipped the tent flap and the tiny window in the opposite end. A mild cross-breeze soon cooled the air and with the sun filtering through the light green tent, bathing everything in a cool soothing pastel, she discovered her morning's anger had dissipated.

"I was beginning to think you were going to sleep the entire day!" Ward's voice said.

Laying on her back on the top of her sleeping bag, she twisted and looked out the door behind her. His Nike-clad feet were just outside. He knelt down, bringing his head a few feet above her own, and for a moment she forgot everything and a smile of genuine welcome lit her face.

"Coffee?" he offered, his voice curiously roughened. She took the cup he held out to her and sipped the lukewarm liquid thankfully, unaware of the intimately appealing picture she made in her sleep-wrinkled clothes and tousled hair.

"How'd you know this is exactly what I'd need?" she asked, then immediately wished she hadn't. His eyes told her she knew quite well how he knew and she lowered her head to the cup again.

"Thanks," she said as he took the empty cup from her hand, his fingers brushing hers. "Let me get changed, and I'll be right out. After riding all night in these clothes and then sleeping in them, I don't think they'll last another minute!"

He brought her the two saddlebags and, as she slowly zipped up the tent flap once more, her eyes followed his muscular frame as he sat down on the picnic bench to wait.

Not being able to stand up in the tent, Stacy had to wriggle into her snug jeans sitting down. Smiling ruefully to herself, she admitted that she'd forgotten the difficulties of dressing while camping. After fastening the last button in the button-up fly of her jeans, she grabbed her embroidered cotton blouse and pulled it over her head. And with socks in one hand and knee-high boots in the other, she carefully walked to the table where Ward was sitting, her bare feet finding small sharp stones with unerring accuracy.

"I couldn't take dressing in there anymore! I felt as if I were folded, ready to be spindled," she said, sitting down next to him on the bench.

"No problem," he said with a grin.

Stacy, leaning over to stuff her narrow-legged jeans into her boots, heard rather than saw his grin and looked up. "Is something—" she began, then stopped when she realized where his eyes were resting with such pleasure. She had neglected to tie the deep V opening of her blouse closed and Ward was obviously enjoying the generous view of her high, firm breasts.

As nonchalantly as she could, she straightened and brought her leg up onto the bench to finish lacing her boots. Then, to divert his attention from her hands as she carefully tied three of the white satiny strands of her blouse, she said, "If you're going to insist on staying . . ."

"We can both go see the sights in my van," he finished for her.

"No!" she cried, standing in front of him, hands on her hips. "Look, Ward, this is my vacation and I'm not going

68

to let you commandeer it! I don't want you here, but since you insist on staying, I'm not going to waste time and energy I need for my photography trying to convince you to leave. But if you are going to accompany me, you'll do it my way!"

"On your motorcycle? Don't be ridiculous! Why do you want to get windblown when we can be comfortable inside my van?"

Before she let herself answer him, she made herself take a deep breath. When that didn't cool the anger that threatened to reemerge, she stalked toward her tent. He might be comfortable with such an arrangement; she certainly wouldn't.

Carefully carrying the boot with her camera equipment toward the BMW, she began fastening the clamps before she finally allowed herself to say, "I don't plan on changing my routine to accommodate your crashing my vacation. If you want to ride behind me on the bike, fine, otherwise, I'll see you later."

She fastened the cuffs of her long-sleeved blouse and put on a light blue Windbreaker. As she was tightening the strap of her helmet, he seemed to finally understand she meant what she said.

"You're serious, aren't you?" When she just gave him a look of disgust, he pointed at the bike, "We can't both fit on that! It's crazy!"

"Suit yourself," she said, pulling on her brown leather gloves. "See you later."

"Wait a minute," he said, his hand going out to detain her, but she quickly shook it off.

The fire in his touch surprised her; she had almost persuaded herself that her earlier reaction to him had merely been an aberration, but the sharp needles of white heat darting through her mocked that idea.

He was the last person she wanted to create such feelings within her! And, picturing them both sitting snugly on the motorcycle, she began to doubt the wisdom of her insistence on his riding behind her. But the thought came too late.

"Okay, I'll ride with you, though God knows why I'm agreeing to it," he said, not bothering to hide his reluctance.

"You don't have to come at all, you know," she said in a last-ditch effort to dissuade him.

Seeing her hesitant figure standing beside the bike, keys dangling from one hand, he looked from the motorcycle seat and back at her. Apparently catching on, he grinned and said, "Too late, honey."

Frowning at his tone, but accepting the inevitable, she threw her leg over the seat and slid the key into the ignition. "The first thing we need to do is try and get you a helmet," she said over the sound of the engine as she reached down to lower the foot pegs for her passenger. "The general store at Furnace Creek might have some."

She leaned forward as he got on behind her. A startled gasp escaped her as his hands automatically went around her waist, but it was overwhelmed by the noise of the engine.

Without having to see him, she could feel his slow smile as he realized the full extent of the situation. Though he could lean back against the padded bar behind him, he allowed her no room and his nearness overpowered her senses as he pressed his body close to hers. The hard muscular frame was molded to hers from her shoulders to her hips and she made a show of adjusting her helmet as she struggled to overcome her intense reaction.

The short trip to the general store was a rough one as she fought the tingling heat that danced through her veins instead of concentrating on shifting smoothly.

Fortunately the store did have a small supply of helmets, in a variety of colors, as long as one wanted black, and Ward was all too soon behind her again as they made their way to the salt flats. The brief respite only served to renew the broiling heat inside her at an even greater intensity than before.

The afternoon in Death Valley was warm—the saleswoman in the store had said it was in the low nineties—but it was nothing compared to the furnace inside Stacy's body Ward was stoking as he lightly held her waist and allowed his fingers to idly caress her.

She could feel the hard muscles of his chest pressed against her back, and she tried to sit straighter to avoid the contact. But his body was wrapped too closely around hers and the friction from her movement only increased the heat in her veins.

How could she have been so stupid? She'd let herself forget that Ward's weapons were never far away. She'd only chosen the battleground, not forestalled the battle.

The season hadn't officially opened yet and the parking area at Badwater was as devoid of other vehicles as the road had been. She hastily dismounted from the bike the minute it rolled to a standstill, anxious to escape Ward's sensuous assault.

She looked up from locking her helmet onto the side of the BMW and found Ward's eyes watching her, his gray gaze soft and warm as it followed her movements.

"You always did have good ideas," he told her, and she

71

had to force herself to look away from the seductive laughter in his eyes.

Forcing herself to smile, she turned and headed for the white path leading through the salt pan.

Standing beside the pool of still water at Badwater, she looked up at the sea-level marker high on a nearby mountain. How appropriate that she was at the lowest point in the continental United States. Her spirits were certainly even lower than the water.

The crunch on the salt told her Ward was approaching, and she turned to watch him. He'd rolled up the cuffs on his casual striped shirt and his smooth informal grace only emphasized his attraction to her. She shivered as she remembered how uncontrollable that attraction had been before.

Following the path out onto the salt flats, Stacy walked slowly with Ward at her side. Her breath came easier when she realized he wasn't going to touch her, and she was able to follow his conversation.

"Why do you keep running away?" he asked abruptly.

Why indeed? Her footsteps punctuated the silence as she strove to find an answer.

"You make me lose control." Stacy shook her head and, before Ward could comment, continued. "No, that's not right—it's more like I don't have any control; I don't lose it so much as forfeit it."

"Is that so bad? With me?"

"Bad? It's terrifying!" Her hands unconsciously rubbed her upper arms as if to ward off a chill. "It feels as if I'm forfeiting not only my control, but my soul . . . my life. And I can't do it, Ward, I just can't do it."

Her words were swallowed by the air as quickly as they were uttered and the strong silence soon defeated her inclination to talk. Alone out in the middle of a salt pan, the silence was complete.

At first she could hear no sounds at all intruding on the two of them. Then her ears grew accustomed to the quiet and she could hear the faint rustle of their breathing mixing curiously with a crackling that seemed to surround them.

Putting her hand up to protect her eyes from the glare of the brilliant white salt, she suddenly realized she was hearing salt crystals cracking in the sun.

She and Ward began their walk back to the motorcycle without exchanging a word, the awesome austere power of the land around them subduing all but their awareness of themselves in a place where time passed on a grander scale than their own short lives.

Once again on the motorcycle, they headed north. It was easier now for Stacy to accept Ward's presence so close behind her and she felt a fleeting hope that the feeling resulted from a profound change within her. But as the distance from the silence of the salt pan increased, her awareness of his body rose in volume.

She felt the rhythmic pressure of his chest from his breathing and she discovered her own breathing had matched his pattern. She deliberately tried to change the pace of her filling lungs, but the seductive caress of his hands on her waist refused to let her concentrate.

One hand lowered to her thigh and rested there while the other remained heating her waist. She felt seared by the contact and she squirmed to free herself, but he did not relinquish his touch. Had it not been for the cooling wind flowing over her, she would have been consumed by the fires raging within.

Turning into the rough side road that led to the Harmony Borax Works, he suddenly tightened his hold on her waist to compensate for the uneven road. She had to shake her head in an attempt to free it from the bonds of fire that started to weld him to her body. She barely waited until Ward had gotten off the bike before jerking it to its kickstand.

She grabbed the motorcycle's boot containing her camera equipment and headed for the tan-colored ruins of the borax works without looking back. After nestling her burden in the scant shade next to one of the remaining walls of the small scattered buildings, she unfolded her tripod and let her photographic eye roam over the scene to find the best angle for her beginning shots.

Ward had been reading the informative signs placed near the parking area, but when he joined her she tensed as the atmosphere became charged with his presence.

"This looks like a good shot from here," he said, pointing to the corner of the low, crumbling wall on which he sat.

"Thanks. I'll check it out in a minute," she promised vaguely as she read the meter of her camera and tried to judge if it represented the best exposure.

"What do you have the camera set on? It's awfully bright isn't it?"

"Hmmm?" she inquired, trying to focus. She raised her head from behind the viewfinder and checked the settings. "F-11 and two hundred fiftieth with a 2-X neutral density . . ." she answered absently.

"Oh," he said with a marked lack of comprehension. "Have you tried that building over there?"

Still bending over the camera, Stacy closed her eyes in irritation. The sounds of a barely whispered "one, two, three" could be heard before she turned to Ward and said in a deceptively calm voice, "No, Ward. I haven't tried that building over there. I may get to it. I may not."

Ward flushed at her tone of almost-too-often tried patience.

"I was just trying to help," he defended.

The bright green flash in her eyes expressed her opinion of his "help" as she said, "If you've discovered a sudden interest in photography, I'm sure we could find you a perfectly adequate Instamatic at the general store."

Silence answered her and she bent back down to her camera.

After an hour, Stacy shot the last frame on her third roll of film and rewound it. Walking to the camera bag to fetch another roll, she saw Ward sitting in the shade of the crumbling wall, his long legs drawn up in front of him. Only his eyes moved as he watched her and she felt a stab of guilt at making him sit there in the heat.

"What do you say we go get something to eat? I'm hungry," she said, packing her camera away and trying not to let her reluctance to leave slow her actions.

Once again in Furnace Creek, they ate a hearty meal at the small restaurant. Stacy, trying to keep the conversation on neutral ground as she made her way through an enormous chef's salad, apologized to Ward for her earlier rudeness.

Ward's smile crept through her guard and she found herself smiling back.

"No, you were right—I was interfering in something I know very little about," he told her, the smile softening as his eyes focused on some midpoint between them. "I used to think that business about someone being 'transported by their art' was so much nonsense, but not after watching

75

you today. I'd never really seen you taking pictures before."

"You saw me taking pictures hundreds of times at the *Beacon!*"

"Never with the intensity you had out there today," he said, his eyes narrowed as if reassessing what they had always shown him. "At the *Beacon,* both our minds were always half on the story. But today, it was . . . different."

Stacy frowned at a particularly innocent strip of cheese. "I'd never thought about it before, I guess. Being 'transported' and all that sounds so trite, but in a way that's what actually happens." She started to carry a forkful of lettuce to her mouth, then halted. Photography had become increasingly important to her over the past five years, but until Ward had put it into words, she hadn't thought about her own responses to it.

"Not physically, of course, but I'll be concentrating on a shot, the light, shadows, imagining the finished picture in my head and trying to—include, I guess I could say—the proper settings on the camera to capture that scene the same way I see it in my head." She tilted her head to one side, lost in her struggle to find the right words to fit the phenomenon.

"I don't know how much time passes when I'm like that, but I do know that suddenly I'll 'pop' back into the present every once in a while and be startled by the sudden awareness of my surroundings." She smiled at him shyly. "I'll bet I'm not making any sense at all."

"You're making a great deal of sense."

His sincerity shone from his eyes with a soft light. From the way he looked at her, she felt a warm contentment steal across her heart, and the first tenuous strands of happiness began to unwind deep within her.

He had always made her think, always forced her to examine and discover aspects of herself she'd only accepted intuitively before. It was with a start that she now realized only Ward had ever made her feel completely alive. Only when he had been beside her, forcing her to strive to reach the very limits of both her mind and body, had she felt the full strength of that happiness.

Unconsciously her eyes returned his smile and his hand reached out to cover hers.

The electricity between them arced from his hand to hers and she jerked her scorched hand back at the shock of it. At the same time she fought to rebuild the breached walls of the protective shell around her heart, but she knew her efforts were weakened by the struggle taking place in the very place she sought to protect. She couldn't afford to let herself be mesmerized by him again!

Shuddering as she recalled how close she had come five years ago to giving in to his strong, seductive pull, she took a long drink of her iced tea to cover the reaction.

"When do you think you'll be going back to the *Monitor*?" she asked him, fear at what his answer would be making her pulse pound. "Robbie probably has a lot more he needs to explain to you."

A look of irritated resignation flashed across his face before he answered her. "Both Roberts and I agree that at this point what I have left to find out can best be learned after I actually take over. And if I have to live through one more of Meeves's meetings, I'll do rude things to one of his CRTs."

Stacy laughed in spite of herself. "He usually stays behind the big oak doors at the other end of the building and doesn't bother us, but every once and a while he has what Clancy calls his 'meeting frenzy.'"

Ward groaned and closed his eyes as if bracing himself for a horrible pronouncement. "And how often do these 'frenzies' occur?"

"Oh, two or three times . . ." she began slowly and grinned at his pained look. ". . . a year."

He gave her a darkling look that promised retribution for her teasing. "I can only hope he'll have gotten over this one by the time I get back."

The grin disappeared from her face in an instant. "And when will that be?" she asked softly.

He shrugged. "Probably not until the end of the week."

She sucked in a thread of breath. Oh, how she wanted to keep on pretending he would be leaving soon, but her pragmatic reporter's mind refused to allow the delusion to continue.

"I'd like to visit Zabriskie Point before it gets too dark," she announced, standing abruptly.

"Stacy," he began, but she was already nearing the door and didn't wait for him to continue.

As her green eyes scanned the upside-down geology of the land spread out below the observation point, every nerve ending was alert to him standing close behind her. The wind was blowing strands of her hair into his face, but when she tried to restrain them, he halted her hand.

Trembling, she moved away from him and went to the motorcycle. She gave the deeply etched gullies of the land in front of her one last glance.

"I'd like to come here at dawn tomorrow and take some pictures."

"Dawn?" he groaned.

"That's when the light's best. Every one of those water-worn crevices will be thrown into sharp relief," she said, pointing eastward. "Early morning and late evening are almost always the best times for photographers. The long, deep shadows give a picture depth and dimension."

Back at their campsites, Ward tried one last tack. "I still don't understand why you have to go up there before dawn just to watch to sun rise. What's wrong with nine or ten o'clock?"

Sighing, Stacy shook her head as she bent down to pour charcoal briquets into the fire ring. She lit the crumpled newspaper under the cone of black squares and made sure it caught before standing and turning to Ward.

"After the sun reaches a certain point in the sky, a scene will look as flat as the paper it's printed on. Shadows add that necessary dimension."

Stacy wanted to explain further, but she'd absently counted the number of hamburgers he was setting out on the wax paper.

"Expecting company?" she asked, counting five patties on the table and another one forming in his hands.

"Just an accompanying side dish of overenthusiasm," he laughed. "It'll go with the potato salad and baked beans."

Returning his smile, she watched him wrap the extra hamburgers. "Lucky you decided to go to the grocery store before following me. If I'm stuck with you, the least you can do is try to appease me with offerings of food!"

"Speaking of which," he said, stepping inside his van. He came out a second later and threw a plastic bag on the table. A few of the tan-colored contents spilled out. "For the high-priestess of photography and sometime charcoal starter."

"Pistachio nuts!" Her hand captured the escaped ones and she immediately began snapping them apart. "Glorious!" she said. "But why would you remember a silly thing like that?"

"How could I forget? For a while there I thought half the food products in the world were green. Not only did you try and stuff me full of vegetables—but your idea of dessert was pistachio-almond ice cream and I even remember a pistachio pudding cake. I could handle the ice cream, but that cake was weird."

She laughed at her innocent attempts to feed him. "I may not have been a nutrition expert, but I knew you needed something!"

"As long as it was green. Am I healthy enough for you now, or are you going to try to restrict my diet again?"

She was kneeling by the fire, unfolding the portable grill he'd brought and, at his question, let her eyes wander over him. Talk about healthy! He chuckled at the slight flush her thoughts had caused and she turned back to the grill.

She tossed another nut into her mouth to cover her embarrassment and walked to the table when he picked up the hamburgers and carried them to the fire. "I think the coals are ready, don't you?" he asked, slapping the meat patties onto the grill.

"Where's the spatula . . . oh, there it is." He reached behind her to pick up the utensil, the side of his body leaning into hers. His lips teasingly nipped her neck.

Moving quickly to get out of his way, she went to the other side of the table and began to dish out the salad and beans. She tried to remember what she had wanted to say, but she was disconcerted to find she had lost her train of thought.

"What did you say?" Ward asked.

"Huh?" she asked, looking up with a delightfully appealing look of confusion. Her neck still burned from his touch and flustered nerves were making her inarticulate.

"I thought you said something."

"Oh. No, no, I didn't say anything." Knowing she was being a complete fool, she frantically searched for something else to say.

"These salads look good," she said, mentally groaning at the high pitch her voice had acquired. "Did you make them?"

"No," he laughed and added in an atrocious French accent, "Chef Fallbrook, he bought zem at ze finest deli een Hannah."

Stacy found herself giggling. "You mean he bought them at the *only* deli in Hannah!"

"You mean that pathetic hole in the wall is *it?*" he asked. Still grinning, she nodded and he frowned at her. "You could try and muster a little bit of sympathy for a poor wretch whose sole source of sustenance for the past five years has been corned beef on rye! What am I going to do?"

"Well, you could try a pistachio." Her grin widened at his look of disgust. "Nothing green, eh? Let's see then. The only place I've seen rye bread is on a patty melt in the coffee shop, but I distinctly remember someone serving corned beef last March—I think it was Clancy."

"Are you saying that for me to get a decent sandwich I'll have to have lunch with Clancy Shaw at Hannah's coffee shop on St. Patrick's Day?"

Laughing aloud, Stacy managed a nod. "Something like that."

"Barbarians! Whatever made you move to such an uncivilized place?!"

The laughter died in her eyes. "I think the hamburgers

81

are done," she said, her voice flat despite the emotions his casual words had reawakened.

Stacy couldn't bring herself to look at him while she carefully placed the whole wheat hamburger buns on the grill to lightly toast, though she knew his gray eyes had narrowed and were following her every movement.

She dreaded his asking her the obvious question, but was also curiously anxious for it. But it wasn't until after he'd thrown a thick blanket onto the ground near the fire and they'd sat down that she was finally able to meet his eyes. She saw the silver laughter had disappeared and they were now an unreadable slate, mirroring her own ambivalence.

She could feel the heat from his body warming hers; their closeness was dictated by the blanket's size. But she said nothing and the long moment of silence stretched on until Ward looked up from his untouched plate and asked softly, "Why Hannah?"

Why shouldn't he know? If she didn't tell him, he would probably figure it out for himself anyway. "After Don was killed, I sent my résumé to every paper in the country that had an opening. The *Monitor* was the first to make an offer, and I took it."

"Just like that? Didn't you look into what kind of paper it was?"

She shook her head. "I didn't care—it was somewhere else than where I was, and that's all that mattered."

Staring into the depths of the leaping flames, Ward slowly chewed a bite of his hamburger and said nothing for a long while. His eyes still on the fire, he asked, "Did Kemble's death affect you so much?"

"Yes, it affected me," she said, watching him crush his empty plastic foam coffee cup at her words. Without knowing why, she took the mangled white pieces from him and threw them on the fire. Over their hissing, she added, "But not how you mean.

"We'd had a fight earlier, but I'd had to go out on assignment that night and had just returned when the sheriff's office called. I couldn't believe he was dead; I kept repeating 'It can't be; it can't be.' Simple shock, grief, hysteria—those I could deal with, but with Don, simple reactions were always out of the question."

"Stacy, I don't want to cause you more pain." He put his arm around her shoulder and, instead of shaking it off, she gratefully leaned into the warm embrace.

"I cursed him again and again. I felt it was so like him to go off and do something calculated to make me feel guilt and shame, to taint my life with his memory." But somehow, that memory was fading now as she became more and more aware of the line of fire where Ward's body touched hers.

"When did you stop loving him?" he asked, his own painful memories making his voice harsh.

"I didn't stop loving him, Ward," she said softly, "because I'd never loved him in the first place."

CHAPTER FIVE

His arm had tensed at the first part of her sentence, though she'd expected to feel him relax when she'd finished. But he surprised her; his arm tightened further and drew her in closer, twisting her body until her breasts were crushed against the hard expanse of his chest.

"Ward . . . I . . ." she said, her stumbling words halted by the violent, angry snap of his eyes that reflected the crackling fire's flames.

Her jacket had opened when he'd pulled her close. With only the thin fabric of their clothes separating them, the hard muscles of his chest teased the tips of her breasts, sparking a current to burn to her very core. Instinctively she lowered her eyes to avoid meeting his hot silver gaze, hoping to hide her growing desire.

He didn't let her escape for long. He bent his fingers under her chin and forced her to look up into the stern, frowning lines of his face. She wanted to tell him that Don wasn't between them anymore, that talking about him had somehow cleansed her, but Ward was beyond listening.

"Honey, you've got no one to run to now," he said harshly, and his mouth descended to hers in a fierce kiss of possession.

Under his onslaught, her mouth opened with little resistance and his tongue mounted its campaign immediately, invading the weakest, most susceptible parts of the moist interior with unrelenting force. She felt his tongue seeking out every intimate hidden crevice, its wet length leaving a trail of desire seeping into her body.

He conquered the sensitive recesses with a devastating sureness, but this assault was only the beginning.

While her own tongue slowly began to respond with a sensual hunger, she could feel his lips tracing the edge of her mouth with a slow deliberation that sparked a more ravenous hunger deep within her.

She could not even pretend to prevent her response to him. The suddenness of his kiss had given her no time to prepare her defenses and now her long-denied need was reveling in his touch. She wanted him. And she knew he knew it when the anger in his kiss began to drain away. But she didn't want to crave this narcotic fire that sped through her veins.

Unable to fight both Ward and her own demanding senses, she tried to call up memories of their last meeting five years before. Surely that vitriolic scene would bring back her sanity. But the only images her mind would form were of remembered fire and laughter.

Unconsciously her hands followed the length of his arms to his shoulders. An involuntary shiver ran through him when her fingers began to play with the tiny curls that had tucked themselves inside his collar at the nape of his neck, and she nipped at his lips in response.

He groaned, his free hand exploring her side through the coarse cotton material of her blouse. With excruciating slowness it rose to cup her breast and she felt as if a beloved friend had come home after too long a separation.

Had she breath left from his kiss, she would have held it in anticipation.

His thumb arced across the fullness of her breast to brush her nipple through her blouse. Back and forth he drew it, making her shake with the intensity of each lightning jolt that shot through her.

Savoring the feel of him, her hands slid beneath his shirt and caressed his muscled back. She reached up to feather his shoulder blades with a light, teasing touch, then drew her fingernails down the strong line in the center of his back to dip tantalizingly inside the waistband of his jeans. The feel of his warm skin was feeding that ball of spinning heat at the core of her womanhood and the familiar, inescapable whirlpool began swirling around her, drawing her down to drown her in her passion.

"My God, what you do to me . . . what you've always done to me," he whispered hoarsely as his lips tasted the perfumed skin below her ear. "I'll have my answers. But not now."

She felt so weakened by her desire that she let herself go limp in his arms. A deep-seated need within her cried out for fulfillment and he responded by flooding her with a torrent of sensations that roared through her veins. The wave of emotion carried her so far that rationality was almost too distant for her to comprehend his words. Almost too far, but not quite.

"Love me, Stacy, just stay and love me," he said, the note of persuasion in his voice telling her he had felt her stiffen.

She felt no anger at him, knowing her own responses were why they had gone so far, but his words had reminded her of her unresolved questions and she leaned back to look up into his face limned in the firelight.

"Why do you fight it?" he asked. "There's so much between us. How can you deny how good we are together?"

"There's too much between us," she said softly, her eyes searching his face for understanding. "Circumstances haven't changed, and neither has the past. I can't block out those years with Don." But even as she said the words, she wondered at their truth; the image of her late husband had seemed a distant memory only a few moments ago.

"Stacy, Stacy," Ward said, gently tracing her jawline with his forefinger, "is it Don, or your body's response to me that you want to block out and can't?" Reading the truth of his words in her eyes, he let his hand drop. "What's the prize in your war against me, against your own body? What battle do you have to win?"

"There's no battle, no war. I'm just not willing to give you that kind of control over me. If I wouldn't give it to you five years ago, I'm doubly against it now. I tried to tell you that earlier, but you wouldn't listen."

"Oh, I listen, I just don't believe it."

"Believe it."

He turned to face the fire, moving away from her to do so. The chill night air moved quickly to fill the space where seconds earlier there had been warmth and comfort. She pulled her jacket closed and crossed her arms in front of her, but it didn't banish the chill inside her.

He lit a cigar, the smoke wafting past her in the darkness after the brilliant flame from his lighter had gone out. She'd noticed that he smoked less than he used to, but he still did when he was stressed and needed time to think.

She started to tell him there was no need for him to stay, but a yawn overrode her words. Weariness had invaded every muscle and bone, and the emotional slackening after reaching such a high pitch earlier had left her drained.

"I seem to recall someone mentioning getting up before dawn tomorrow," Ward chuckled. "Why don't you go on to bed, honey. I'll see you in the morning."

"Ward, you don't have to—"

"To bed! Dawn waits for no photographer," he said, rising and walking her to her tent. Before she ducked through the tent flap, his arms surrounded her and drew her close for a gentle hug. His lips brushed her forehead for an instant before he let her go.

Alone in her tent, she undressed quickly and snuggled down into the sleeping bag. She drew it tightly around her, trying not to regret that it wasn't the warmth of his arms embracing her instead.

Her body ached for him. Visions from the past mocked her, visions of Ward's hard, virile body stretching next to hers after they'd made love. Even the memory of him made her respond, and she quickly turned over on her stomach, forcing the images away. She could never let him know how much he still affected her.

Finally she heard the door to his van open and then close. She resolved to keep him at arm's length tomorrow, but the resolutions melted away with her consciousness when sleep overcame her.

It seemed only a few hours later that the tiny quartz alarm was chirping her awake. After she had stumbled to and from the shower building with the aid of a flashlight, she longingly thought of a cup of coffee, but a glance at the dark turquoise of the horizon told her she probably didn't have enough time to fix it.

She began checking her camera equipment by the weak beam from the flashlight, making sure everything would be ready to go once the sun put in an appearance. While she was trying to set the ISO rating on her camera in the faint light, the door to Ward's van opened and he appeared, obviously showered and dressed to accompany her. But her eyes only noticed that in passing; the real object of her gaze was the steaming cup in his right hand.

"Oh, that smells good," she said.

He took a sip and walked closer to the table. "I'd offer you a cup, but . . ."

"Thanks, I'd love one."

"Sure you have time?" He took another sip.

Stacy licked her lips, her eyes never leaving the white cup. "I think I could manage a swallow or two."

"Okay, if you're sure. I'm not sure if I've got any creamer though," he said.

"I'll take it black," she said in a rush.

Ward laughed and handed her his cup. "Here, if you're that desperate, take mine. I think it's cool enough to drink."

Without another word she took several gulps from the cup he'd handed her. Her eyes closed and she leaned her head back, a long sigh of satisfaction escaping her. At his delighted laugh, she opened her eyes and smiled self-consciously.

"I'm absolutely pitiful before my first cup of coffee."

"So I noticed," he said. "I'll have to remember that the next time I need to wring a concession or two out of you."

"Beastly. Taking advantage of a deranged woman like that."

"But effective."

"I don't know about that. Isn't there something about promises made under duress?"

"Not promises made to me," he said with an enigmatic smile that made her want to change the subject quickly.

"I think we'd better get going. The sun's going to rise and I won't be there to catch it!"

"That's my Stacy—always running to catch the sun."

They arrived at Zabriskie Point before the sun had broken over the distant mountains and Stacy was ready when it did. With swift, concentrated motions, she took picture after picture of the dramatically shadowed land, her hand unconsciously changing the aperture and shutter speed to produce her mental image of the scene.

Finishing the last shot on her fourth roll of film, she turned to find Ward watching her intently. When he didn't answer her questioning look, she turned back to the convoluted landscape but decided that the best time for photographs had already passed.

She began to pack her equipment back in the padded boot on her motorcycle when Ward's hand brushed a chestnut curl from her forehead and she stopped.

"Do you know how beautiful you are?" he asked, his voice low and vibrant. "When you're working, your eyes turn gold with concentrated energy." His finger traced the bone under her eye, as if to absorb some of that energy.

Tendrils of some unknown feeling wrapped around her limbs, holding her to the place where she stood. She found her eyes dropping from his magnetic gaze to his lips, watching in fascination as they came nearer to hers.

She braced herself for the explosive force of his kiss and was unprepared for the reverent gliding softness of the tiny ridges of his lips gently rasping against hers. Having been ready for a demanding kiss of desire, she was rocked by his subtle passion and it left her no choice but to cling to him until her reeling equilibrium restored itself.

When he lifted lips from hers, she gave an inaudible whimper at her loss, and for a moment could do nothing but stare up at him.

Shakily she finished packing her camera equipment and closed the lid on the boot. What had happened? How could a gentle kiss have altered her so? She looked around her. Nothing was as it had been; all her perceptions had been changed. All her convictions had been knocked from their niches and lay in shards at the bottom of her mind.

Daring to look up into the gray tapestry of his eyes, she was once more woven into their spell and, suspended from her earlier resolutions, her eyes closed in anticipation of his kiss.

He tasted her lips again, savoring their sweet softness until she felt the rising tension in him. His tongue began to follow the inner contour of her lips, dipping inside to the glistening wetness in quick teasing motions that left her wanting more. When he held back from deepening the kiss, she took the initiative, daring to lead him where her passion would have them go.

She let her own tongue slip inside to his inner lips, trailing along the line of his teeth. Skimming her tongue over the surface of his inner cheeks with mounting desire, she then plunged deep into the moist vault of his mouth, eager to taste all he had to offer. Sensing his surprise, she continued her journey until his response began to answer her.

With a suddenness born of the shivering, thrumming demand in the center of her being, she began a sensual joust which she knew would end in the unseating of all her rational reservations.

But she was saved from her surrender by the sound of

a car driving up the steep entrance road into the parking lot overlooking the Point. Hastily pulling apart, they stood staring at each other while they gulped in lungfuls of air to calm their raging blood. She drew back her hands, which had been unconsciously kneading the taut muscles at his shoulders.

"What do you say we go get some breakfast?" she asked, getting on the motorcycle, her shaken composure evident in her voice.

Clearing his throat as he got on the bike behind her, he settled in and slowly let his hands encircle her waist.

"Fine," he said. He cleared his throat again.

Little was said while they prepared breakfast back at the campsite. Ward cooked the eggs, bacon, and toast on the stove in his van and Stacy readied the picnic table and poured the orange juice. He'd suggested they eat at the small dinette inside, but when she shook her head, he accepted her refusal without demur.

Lingering over their breakfast, they were both reluctant to discuss anything while the kiss at Zabriskie Point was still a palpable force between them. Her shattering reactions to that kiss left no doubt where her emotions and desires were leading her—to disaster.

She felt no anger at the situation, but a cold lump of fear had settled in her stomach and she frantically searched for a tactful way to ask Ward to leave.

Had they been in the newsroom all this time, she knew her resolve would not now be wavering so precariously. There the barriers between them would be easier to put up and maintain. But here that deep attraction that had once bound them so thoroughly, coupled with her own undeniable desire for him, was ruthlessly eroding the foundation of the artificial wall she'd erected.

"Ward, we've got to stop and think where all this is leading us," she said, hoping to approach the subject of his leaving obliquely.

"We both know where it's leading us," he answered, his fingers idly stroking the back of her hand as it lay on the stone surface of the picnic table. "Back to where we belong —with each other."

She withdrew her hand from his touch and put it in her lap where her nervous fingers began plucking at the edge of the paper napkin.

"You don't understand! It's leading us nowhere! Play the scene out, Ward, and in the end you'll find an empty stage." Her hand came back to the table, her fingernails thrumming against the cool surface in her agitation.

"Not an empty stage," he answered, "but a full, loving, happy life together."

"What are you saying?" she asked, a hysterical edge creeping into her voice. But she didn't need to ask; she could already feel the restricting chains of commitment twining around her. Why wouldn't he accept that she didn't want to have any kind of relationship with him but a professional one? Just because she reacted to his sensual barrage didn't mean she wanted to!

"What do you think I'm saying? I want us to be together alwa—"

"No!" she cried, then added more calmly, "No, please, please, don't say it." She blinked away the tears of panic filling her eyes. Her words started to spill out rapidly, the fear inside absorbing her. "You don't understand. We are not going to be together—not now, not ever."

"How can you say that after last night, and especially after the way you kissed me!" he demanded.

"I've seen what happens to people when they say 'Oh,

we'll be together forever!' and go gaily tripping to the altar. As soon as you say yes, the bars to your cage start going up. Suddenly what was wonderful is now a flaw. What was once acceptable is now condemned. There you are, day after day, hour after hour, living with subtle—and not so subtle—hints to change. You're pressed to fit into a mold that's not your size."

"Stacy, you know I wouldn't—"

"Know you wouldn't what? Want me to change? Hah!" she said, jumping to her feet. Tiny puffs of dusts hovered near the ground with each nervous step, her hands wringing as the pent-up emotions began spilling over the carefully constructed walls of her memory. "You remember Don? Whenever I'd go out with him, he'd introduce me to anyone he'd recognize, making sure they knew I was a reporter. He'd even mention stories I'd written. 'Did you read that article on the problems at the dam construction site? Stacy here wrote it!' He'd practically be beaming at me."

"And you were upset when he stopped?" Ward asked, a puzzled frown on his face.

Unpleasant laughter escaped her. Raking her hand through her hair, she answered. "If it had stopped, maybe it would have been easier to deal with the rest of it. But it didn't. He kept on lavishly praising me in public, making everyone think my being a reporter was the most important thing in his life."

She stopped and leaned toward him, her hands resting on the edge of the table. "But you know what was *really* important to him? Having dinner on the table at six sharp —right when I was due at a city council meeting. Or he'd be screaming at me for leaving in the middle of the night to go cover a big warehouse fire."

Pacing again, the morning sun made the red lights in her hair dance with each agitated step. "And do you know why he'd stomped out of the house the night his car ran off the road? He'd flown into a rage because he couldn't find one of his favorite socks. Couldn't find a goddamned sock!"

She was shaking now and tears fell down her face unchecked. Ward came to her and pulled her into his arms, but though his hands stroked and comforted her body, his words inflamed her anger.

"Stacy, did Don ever work again as a reporter or photographer after that stunt he pulled at the *Beacon?*"

She shook her head but her body tensed, waiting for his next words.

"Then don't you think he might have acted the way he did because of jealousy? How do you think he felt watching his wife continue as a respected member of the same profession from which he was banned?"

She wrenched out of his embrace. "I should have known you'd defend him! Take his part against mine!" Her hands balled into fists at her side and they itched to pummel his broad, arrogant chest.

"I'm not taking his side," Ward told her, struggling to keep his voice even. "I was only suggesting that maybe it wasn't marriage or any kind of commitment that made him act that way, but his own disappointment and envy." He started to walk toward her again with his arms extended, but she backed away.

Fierce irrational anger was clouding her vision and muffling her hearing. She hadn't heard his explanation, but even if she had, the words would not have penetrated through the thick veil of distress her memories of Don had created.

"Don't touch me," she said, her tone low and menacing. Her chest was heaving from the deep gulps of air her lungs were drawing in, and the edge of her vision was starting to shimmer red.

"I didn't want to make you angry," he said, obviously not understanding her frustration at his not realizing the depth of her feelings. "Let's go to the Sand Dunes as we'd planned. We can talk later, okay?"

A prickling grayness began to tease her senses and she felt faint. She was finally able to slow her breathing, and sitting down on the bench in front of the abandoned remains of her breakfast, she said, "No. You go. I want to stay here for a while."

"I don't think I should leave you alone," he said slowly. "We can go later in the day."

"No, please go," she said, her anger dissipating, his lack of understanding leaving only a dull pain near her heart. Now all she wanted to do was be alone and reweave the fragile, torn fabric of her self-control.

She looked away from the concern on his face. "I need to be alone for a while—I'll be all right. To be honest, I'd take my motorcycle somewhere, but I don't feel up to it."

He sat down beside her on the bench but did not touch her. "If you're sure that's what you want, I'll go on to the Sand Dunes by myself. But I'll be back in about an hour to see how you're doing."

She watched him stand, her eyes following the play of muscles over his body at the movement. A stab of regret at their argument pierced her, but she quickly shrugged the pain away.

At her nod of agreement, his eyes left hers to scan the almost empty campground. It was still a couple of weeks before the season officially opened and only one other site

96

was taken. His gray gaze rested for a moment on the enormous RV parked in the lower level near the entrance, apparently weighing its threat.

He must have decided it was benign, for he squeezed her shoulder and said, "Take care, honey. I'll see you in an hour or so."

A gust of wind blew across the table, sending the paper plates from breakfast scattering to the ground. The noise startled Stacy out of her trance and she quickly gathered up the trash and threw it away.

She had no idea of how long she had been sitting on the bench in a stupor. A glance at her watch told her it was nearing noon, and she tried to recall when Ward had left. She frowned. Whatever time it had been, he surely should have returned by now. Hadn't he said he'd be back in an hour? Instinctively she knew it had been much longer than that.

Her eyes were drawn to the empty driveway next to her campsite. Had he gone to the Furnace Creek restaurant for lunch, thinking she needed more time to recover? No doubt that's what happened.

Still frowning, she unconsciously began rolling up the sleeves of her white eyelet blouse and then undid another button. She'd never been to Death Valley this early before; it certainly was hot.

The heat! Ward had said he'd never been here before, but surely he wasn't still out in the Sand Dunes. Was he? Grabbing her motorcycle helmet, she was on the BMW in a minute and heading down the narrow winding road that led out of the campground to the highway.

Just to make sure she wasn't headed on a fool's errand, she made a quick inspection of the restaurant's parking lot, but didn't see his TransVan. Heading north again, she revved up the bike. Ignoring the orange arrow that told her just how fast she was speeding, she kept looking ahead to make sure she didn't miss the turnoff for the dunes.

Visions of Ward suffering from sunstroke haunted her. Staying out in the sun too long was no laughing matter, but could cause serious illness and, occasionally, death.

When she finally turned onto the gravel road that led to the parking lot at the Sand Dunes, she could see the TransVan. She didn't have time to enjoy the stark beauty of the hills of blowing sand, but instead concentrated on what she might find ahead.

Braking to a halt in a spray of stones, she was off her bike in an instant and pounding on the door of the van, but a quick look through the window told her he wasn't inside.

Oh, God, he was still out on the dunes! Frantically looking about her, she saw one set of footprints leading up the nearest hill and without thinking ran toward them. But halfway up she stopped and ran back down to her motorcycle to grab one of the canteens.

Bounding to the dunes, she once again began running up the hill of sand. She was panting by the time she reached the top, her feet sinking past her ankles in the loose, flowing sand with each step making her climb doubly difficult.

Putting her hand to her forehead to shield her eyes from the glare of the sand, she searched for any sign of Ward. There were a few scattered bushes near the parking lot, but after those only the undulating hills and the mountains beyond. And she saw nothing else.

Hurrying to the crest of another hill, a dark patch interrupted the tan expanse to her left and she immediately set off in that direction. As she neared it, she realized it was indeed Ward, partially hidden by another dune. She also realized that he was moving toward her, slowly, jerkily, occasionally falling, but still moving.

"WARD!" she cried, using every ounce of air in her lungs to bellow across the sand. He stopped and looked up, his hand going up in a weak wave. She took off again at a run, not noticing when she half-walked, half-slid down a dune to him.

"My God," she said, sitting down next to him and opening the canteen in one movement. "Just take a sip . . . don't gulp it, or you'll get sick."

Now that she was next to him, she could see he wasn't as ill as she'd thought. He'd wisely tied his handkerchief on his head, letting part of it hang down to cover his face.

"Thanks," he said, pouring water on the cloth over his head before handing the canteen back to her. "Ah, am I glad to see you."

"Can you walk? We're really not too far from the van." She helped him stand, staggering a little when he stumbled and his full weight fell on her.

"I'll be fine once I get out of this sun. God, it's hot," Ward said, his words coming slowly. "I never thought it would get this hot in October."

"It is Death Valley. But let's get going; it's ridiculous to stand out here and discuss the weather."

The walk back to the van was slow, with Ward stumbling several more times. One of her arms was around his waist while the other held his arm around her shoulder. When they slid down the last hill to the parking lot, she thought nothing had ever appeared so beautiful as the TransVan did at that moment.

"I think I left the back door unlocked," he said.

Entering the van, she realized this was the first time she'd been in it, but she didn't have time to notice the tiny galley just inside the door or the small comfortable dinette.

Ward immediately sprawled on the long sofa opposite the table that had been left made up into a bed. He leaned back against the top sheet, reveling in the comparative coolness of the shaded interior.

"Here, drink this," Stacy told him, handing him a glass of orange juice. "I wish you had some Gatorade, but this'll have to do."

While he drank the orange liquid slowly, she fiddled with the controls on the air-conditioning unit until she felt a stream of cool air blowing in.

"That feels good," he said, opening his shirt to let the air flow over his chest. "But can't you lower the temperature some more?"

"No, you can't go from one extreme temperature to another. Your body will cool off soon." She gently undid the handkerchief and took it off. Since he'd thought to have that covering, he was only slightly sunburned, but Stacy knew he probably had one fierce headache. "How's your head?"

"Ghastly. Who'd think that walking in the sunshine could make your head feel like some malevolent blacksmith's anvil."

"That bad, huh?" she asked, and got a groan in response. "Well, if your stomach handles the orange juice all right, I'll give you some aspirin later on."

"I don't mean to complain, but I still feel like hell. You sure you won't turn that thing lower?"

"No," she said, wishing she could do something else to help him. Then an image flashed in her mind of a friend

100

bathing her infant son in cool water to help ease a fever. "But I know what I will do. Take off your shirt."

A dark eyebrow went up. "Honey, I hate to say it, but I really don't think I'm up to it right now."

With a look of exasperation she bent down and finished unbuttoning his shirt. "For God's sake, I know you haven't had a pleasant experience, but that doesn't mean you're helpless."

"Well, if you insist . . ." he said, pulling her to him.

"Ward! What *are* you doing?"

"Showing you I'm not helpless," he said with a smile in his voice. His hands caressed the smooth silk of her skin under her blouse and she swayed into him. But she jerked back when she felt the intense heat from his body.

"You're burning up!" she cried, breaking away from his embrace.

"You noticed," he said dryly. "But then I always am around you."

She hunted through the cupboard and pulled out a towel. "Be serious! Why didn't you tell me you were still so hot! That could be dangerous."

After she soaked the towel in the sink and wrung it out, she carried it to the bed. He'd finally taken off his shirt and laid down on his stomach.

He drew in his breath over his teeth as the cool cloth contacted his skin, but then she felt him relax. Without thinking, she let her eyes travel over the wide expanse of his muscled back as her hand drew the towel over it. She remembered how the silken steel of his skin had felt under her hands the night before, and she shifted uncomfortably on the edge of the bed.

Her tongue flicked out to moisten her suddenly parched lips. Shifting again, she brought the towel near his waist, though her eyes drifted lower to the twin firm mounds above his powerful thighs. She longed to let her hand slide over those inviting curves, but he stirred when her hand had ceased moving the towel and she quickly went back to her task. Talk about getting overheated!

"There was something important I had to tell you," he said, mumbling into the pillow with the last of his strength. "I had forgotten, but I remembered out there. Remembered about your mother . . ."

"Shhh," she said gently, smoothing his hair with her fingertips. She couldn't distinguish his words and was tempted to ask him to repeat them, but she knew it wasn't the time for conversation. "We can talk later, Ward, just rest for now," she crooned.

She cooled his shoulders and neck once more and stood up. The regular rise and fall of his torso told her he was close to sleep. Reaching down to shift the pillow under him to a more comfortable position, she glanced out the large window above him and suddenly remembered they were still in the parking lot of the sand dunes.

Should they stay here or go back to the campground? Biting her lower lip while she considered the options, she came to a decision and her hand went out to Ward's sleeping form.

Sliding her fingers into the jeans' pocket nearest her, she silently pleaded for his keys to be there. She could feel the hard muscles of his thigh through the cotton lining of the pocket and she willed herself not to think of where her hand really was.

He stirred once again but, now deep in sleep, it was only to shift his position—fortunately to the side that exposed more of his pocket and she was able to reach in farther until her fingers felt the cold serrated edge of a key.

Withdrawing them in triumph, she held on to them tightly as she left the van and went to lock up her motorcycle. She hated to leave it, but at the moment she couldn't think of any alternative other than to drive the van back to the campsite. Besides being at a higher—and cooler—elevation, help was nearby in case his condition worsened.

After checking Ward a final time, she sat down in the van's driver's seat and put the key into the ignition. Seeing the BMW dwindle to a speck in her side mirror, she felt a queasy stirring of emotions, as if she were watching a part of herself disappear from view. So many emotions had been born and reborn that day . . . could she ever go back to the way she'd been before Ward had reentered her life?

CHAPTER SIX

Ward woke briefly when she pulled into the campsite, but she soon soothed him back to sleep. She had driven slowly to avoid throwing him about on the bed at each turn; what he needed most now was to continue his healing sleep.

Sitting at the dinette across the narrow aisle from Ward's sleeping form, she was making notes about her photographic session at Zabriskie Point when the early afternoon sun slashed over his face and woke him.

"What time is it?" he asked, his words slurred from sleep.

"Going on two. How are you feeling?" She turned, sitting sideways on the upholstered bench, her knees in the aisle, and bent over to peer into his face. Her fingers stroked the magnificent shoulder nearest her, testing its warmth. "You feel cooler."

He tried to lick his lips, but the inside of his mouth was as dry as the outside. "I need a glass of water." He started to rise, but Stacy put out a restraining hand.

"Lie still; I'll get it for you."

"Now I know how all those old stereotyped prospectors felt croaking for water," he said, accepting the glass she held out to him.

"Not so fast," she warned.

His gulping slowed somewhat, but he quickly finished the glass. Handing it back to her, he said, "Did you ever notice how nothing tastes as sweet as water when you're dying of thirst?"

"I know exactly what you mean; I got a little dry out there myself." She pulled out a tiny white jar from her purse and handed it to him. "Put some of this on your lips. It'll keep them from chapping."

He looked at it suspiciously, his hands remaining at his sides. "It looks like makeup. Are you turning kinky on me?"

A sound halfway between a laugh and impatience escaped her. "Don't be ridiculous. It's only lip gloss—clear, no perfume, and it has all sorts of moisturizers in it. And if you don't believe you need it, try smiling once."

His lips stretched horizontally a fraction in a tentative test. "All right, you win. But isn't there any ChapStick?"

"If I had any, I'd offer it to you. Now, here." She held the jar out to him again.

"Wait! Did you check the first aid kit? I think there's some Vaseline in it."

Sighing, she put the lip gloss on the table, the jar landing with a sharp crack. "What first aid kit?"

"The one in the cupboard up there," he said, pointing appropriately.

She dutifully dug out the plastic case and set it on the table. "Let's see, first aid cream—I don't think that would work for lips—inhalants, hmmmm, I don't see . . . wait a minute, here's some packets of something. Darn, just antiseptic towelettes." Shaking her head, she started to put the kit away when an olive green oval caught her eye. Surely no one would put Vaseline in a snakebite kit. "Ah ha! Success at last. Here you are, sir, one battered packet of Vaseline with the print chipping off."

He started to grin, then quickly stopped when his tender lips protested. "Thanks."

Once the shiny ointment was in place, he experimented on its effect by pulling his mouth in grimaces and smiles and once it formed a wide *O* when an unexpected yawn caught him unawares.

The glistening mobile mouth tantalized her and she stood watching him, entranced. Stacy told herself to calm down, but the sun glittering off the soft vertical ridges of his lips mocked her feeble resolve.

"I was prepared for it to be hot, but the dryness was a surprise," he said, his voice bringing her out of her stupor. "I feel as if I were made out of dried leather."

His hand rubbed along his forearm to emphasize the point, the undulating muscles of his bare chest inviting her touch. To her, he looked tanned and healthy, though still a bit tired. If his skin was like dried leather, it was certainly a soft sensuous suede.

"With as little rain as Death Valley gets in a year, you could hardly have been expecting the Everglades."

"No," he chuckled, "but to know someplace is dry because you've read it in a book is vastly different from feeling it."

"Does this mean *adieu*?" She grinned when he gave her a look of disgust. "I'd settle for *au revoir*."

"Dream on, honey. I'm here for the duration; I was merely commenting on the weather."

Though his words were filled with all the insouciance he could have hoped for, Stacy saw him struggling with a yawn. She realized with a guilty start that he wasn't nearly as recovered as he'd tried to make her believe. And when

106

he turned to look out the window, surreptitiously rubbing his forehead, she rushed to make amends.

"Let me get you some aspirin," she said, retrieving the first aid kit.

"No, I'm fine. But thanks."

She stood over him, blatantly using her temporary advantage in height. "Sure, you're fine," she told him with teasing sarcasm. "That's why I don't keep seeing you keep rubbing your temples, and those two furrows in your forehead deep enough to plant corn in are figments of my imagination."

His hand had immediately stopped its rubbing and fallen to his lap. "You're making too big a deal out of a little headache," he said, a touch of belligerence texturing his voice.

Sighing, she measured out two tablets and refilled his glass with water. Ward did not like to be fussed over when he was ill; he couldn't stand weaknesses of any sort. But Stacy couldn't sit by and watch him suffer because of his pride. A little gentle bullying was called for.

"As fond of children as I am, I didn't plan on spending my vacation cajoling a recalcitrant three-year-old into taking his medicine," she said, careful to keep her voice light and teasing.

He gave in grudgingly and took the aspirin, drinking the entire glass of water for his reward.

"Why don't you try resting some more," she said, taking his glass. When he appeared reluctant, she added, "Nothing burns energy out of you faster than heat and wind, and you had an ample dose of both."

He took her advice and she watched his supine form lose its tenseness to sleep. She returned to her notes, but other thoughts intruded and the cryptic messages blurred in front of her.

Their isolation was wreaking its own kind of destruction on her resistance. She realized now, too late, that she should have insisted he return to Hannah immediately— no matter what. She would have been able to maintain her distance at the *Monitor*.

Her eyes were unconsciously watching his light, even breathing and she forced herself to shift her gaze out the window. But they weren't at the *Monitor*. They were alone and together in a place where natural forces made her protestations seem insignificant and trivial. The place invited introspection and an intimacy that was hard to deny.

Frowning at the trend of her thoughts, she forced her mind back to her notes.

It was nearing dusk when Stacy felt an odd sensation along the back of her neck. Looking around to Ward, she discovered him half-sitting on the sofa, watching her with an unreadable expression in his eyes. The sheet had fallen to his waist, but she forced her eyes to remain level with his gaze.

"Are you feeling better?" she asked, hoping the uneasiness his intent look was causing didn't come through in her words. She turned in her seat to face him, her knees filling up the aisle.

"Much. Thanks for insisting on that last nap—and the aspirin," he said. He sat up straight and swung his legs over the edge of the bed, resting them alongside hers.

"Did you leave your motorcycle at the sand dunes?" he asked, knowing the answer. "We can drive back and get it; I'm up to that at least."

"It'll be all right in the parking lot," she said, her doubt obvious.

"Look, all I have to do is sit down in the driver's seat and aim the van. Nothing to it," he said.

She looked at him closely. "You seem to be better. I guess we could go get it, but you have to promise to lie right back down as soon as we get back."

The trip took longer than she'd expected, and after she'd parked her motorcycle in the campsite next to his, she went back into the van and discovered Ward already back on the sofa. She sat down in the dinette across from him.

"I don't know about you, but I'm starving," she said with only the slightest quiver in her voice. "After a little breakfast and no lunch . . ."

He propped up the pillow behind him and leaned back, putting his legs back into the aisle. "You're right; make mine rare."

"Your what?"

"My steak, of course. Maybe some fried potatoes on the side and a nice big spinach salad."

"Dream on. You couldn't begin to handle that stuff yet. What you're going to get is a vegetable and cheese omelet."

He grimaced at the plain fare. "I'll concede, but only because you chose to attack when I'm weak with hunger," he said with an air indicating he was fading away. But he was quickly sitting upright again. "Don't forget the mushrooms; an omelet's not an omelet if it isn't smothered in sauteed mushrooms."

She rose and went to the tiny galley and began searching the cupboards. Pulling out a skillet and a long, sharp knife, she asked, "Is Chef Fallbrook going to cook or sit quietly on the sidelines until the food's done?"

"Executive Chef Fallbrook is going to direct the sou-chef in the proper way to make a superb, substantial omelet."

Giving him a withering glance, she opened the refrigerator and said, "I don't believe it. You've got two tomatoes, three carrots, an onion, four potatoes, and a bag of mushrooms; no broccoli, no celery, no avocados. Nothing that could be called green."

"Avocados are borderline; sometimes they're yellow inside."

"Wait a minute! Spinach is green, and you wanted a spinach salad not five minutes ago."

"All right, I'll admit it. I do like raw spinach and I've been known to sample an artichoke or two."

She pulled out a cutting board and began washing and slicing the vegetables. "I don't remember your being so, umm, particular."

"I hadn't learned to be assertive yet."

"You? Unassertive? Hah!" she told him, chopping the carrots with a punctuating *wham!* of the knife with each slice. "I certainly don't remember you making such a fuss about it. Maybe it's just my selective memory."

"I doubt if we discussed vegetables much; we were too busy doing other things . . ." His words trailed off while his eyes scanned her from toes to curls.

Stacy flushed and a quarter of the onion was minced very fine beneath her knife. Their easy camaraderie, so like what they'd had during their days at the *Beacon,* had lulled her and the blatant reminder of their earlier relationship threw her off-guard.

Her laugh was brittle. "No, we didn't talk about vegetables. We'd talk about saving the world from itself, preventing war and disease and poverty." She stopped to brush away the moisture in her eyes. The rivulets of tears making their way down her face were strictly from the onion; she certainly couldn't be regretting her earlier fanciful notions of political theory. "I'd forgotten how silly young . . ."

". . . lovers," he finished. Her knife stopped in mid-descent; everything about the way he said the word, its modulation, its tone, the very depth of its source, sparked an answering response in her she couldn't deny.

Stacy resumed preparing their dinner, but there was always that memory of the way they'd once been hanging between them, a vivid arousing remembrance of the heights they'd climbed together.

Butter sizzled in the skillet and the next few minutes were spent sauteing the vegetables, including a generous handful of sliced mushrooms. When she had swirled the creamy yellow eggs around the pan and let them cook to a golden brown, she spooned the vegetable mixture onto one-half of the omelet and expertly flipped it into thirds out onto a plate.

"Dinner is served," she said, placing the plate down in front of Ward. He'd moved from the sofa to the dinette while she'd been cooking. Now he speared a tomato slice that garnished the top of the omelet while he waited for her to join him.

Dinner was a tense affair for Stacy. He watched every bite she took, his eyes resting on her lips as she opened her mouth to take each morsel. She chewed self-consciously and quickly lost any hope of tasting her food.

He had not put his shirt back on for the meal—she assumed he was still too hot—and time and again her own eyes strayed to the wide expanse of his gleaming naked chest. His golden skin undulated with each muscle as he raised his glass to drink or brought a forkful of food to

111

disappear behind his even white teeth. Her hands ached to follow the movements.

When her omelet was half-finished, she pushed it away from her, her earlier hunger gone. It had been replaced by another kind of hunger, the kind that could only be sated by the man sitting across from her. To cover her growing desire, she took their plates to the tiny galley and rinsed them. She too washed up, hoping the cool water would douse the flames that were beginning to singe her. Sitting back down again, she was aghast to find herself almost shaking with her need to feel his body under her hands— and he hadn't even touched her!

He washed up in silence and sat down on the sofa directly across from her, his knees filling the aisle. She put her elbows on the table and crossed her arms, a pitiful attempt at a nonchalant smile creasing her face.

She knew he sensed her mood and she desperately wanted to escape to her tent. But when his hand reached out and caressed her shoulder, the electric touch convinced her that she had done too much running where Ward was concerned. Besides, at the moment she doubted whether she was capable of moving away from him at all.

"Thank you for the dinner, honey," he said. His hand tightened slightly and he pulled her to him. She felt herself moving toward him, his magnetic attraction drawing her to him with the slightest of physical pressure.

She sat close beside him and his warm breath feathered her ear when he added, "You were right—it was just what I needed." His hand began to move slowly up and down her upper arm, the friction sending sparks spinning through her blood.

Along her shoulders she felt the muscles in his arm tense. With a gentle, slow, inexorable tightening, he drew her to him and she discovered a sensuous lethargy had settled over her, making her powerless to resist.

His lips closed on hers and she knew nothing else but his touch and the consuming fires within. He leaned back on the sofa-bed, drawing her down over him until the entire length of her body was pressed intimately into his. The devastation his tongue was wreaking in the warmth of her mouth was echoed in every place her soft flesh yielded to his hard masculine frame.

Warm hands caressed the small of her back while they pressed her even farther into the hard length of his body, the evidence of his growing desire unmistakably firm against her. One of his hands traveled upward to steady her shoulders as their kiss deepened and the other lowered to the soft round double swell of her derrière to delight in the yielding flesh beneath the fabric of her jeans.

Unable to ignore the urging deep within her, her own hands were traveling down the hot flesh of his arms to caress the curve of his narrow waist. Her fingertips played a silent melody of desire over the taut muscles of his shoulders, the contrast between the satin surface of his skin and the iron straps of muscle beneath driving all thoughts of resistance to the farthest corners of her mind.

She felt the coolness of the sheet beneath him, but it failed to halt her spiraling passion. Her arms returned his demanding embrace and in a far corner of her mind a distant, rational Stacy stood aghast at her compliance. But after his teeth tugged at her earlobe, his tongue followed the curve of her ear, sending the teasing nips of a sensual chill down her spine and the tiny image was gone from view when the whitecaps of another passionate wave engulfed it.

"Ahhh," she gasped, feeling the hot insistence of his

manhood pressing into her. He shifted under her, and his supine length completely covered the van's bed. The minute form of her rational mind reappeared all too briefly.

"Ward, no," she said thickly, the roiling passion in her veins making it difficult to form her words even as she levered herself up enough so their chests were no longer in contact. "I'm not ready for this. . . ." But she couldn't continue; her body's need for him refused to let her finish. Intent only on its fulfillment, that need made her ignore the commitment implicit in what she was doing.

And she knew Ward had deliberately not listened to her words. His hand stroked the back of her thigh, his fingers brushing upward to the intimate source of her desire to feel the heat his touch had caused.

She gasped and pushed against him farther until his hand left the burning thigh and followed the contour of her body up under her blouse, the long-heated trail on her side ending when his thumb encountered the steep swell of her breast. With a gentle back-and-forth motion, his thumb slowly but inexorably made its way to the rose-colored peak and she held her breath in anticipation.

The hardening summit of her breast grew toward his hand in an unmistakable appeal for him to continue. She was unable to stifle a sigh of protest when he interrupted the swirling pad of his thumb to remove her blouse. But the tenseness inside her continued to increase, and when his hands encircled her and drew her down to nestle between him and the back of the sofa, she didn't resist.

They rested for a moment, each breathing deeply to regain a bit of their lost equilibrium. Ward's lips brushed her forehead, a cooling counterpoint to the searing contact of their nude torsos. At first she was confused at his stopping, but the kiss told her that he had heard her protest and he was giving her time to pull back from what would surely follow if they continued. But even the echo of her protest had disappeared, and her hand traced the thatch of dark curls on his chest down to the belted waist of his jeans.

She felt his lungs pull in air when her fingers began to unbuckle his belt. His muscles tensed and his hand came up to lightly cover hers, stopping her momentarily. "Are you sure, honey?"

She could no longer deny her desire for him and her lips pressed into the hollow of his shoulder in reassurance. Then the only sound in the van was the rattle of his brass belt buckle when she freed it, her fingers immediately dipping beneath the waistband to unsnap his jeans. Her hand continued its downward task and soon his zipper was completely undone.

She could feel the heat of his desire beneath her hand as her fingers slipped under the worn blue denim. Time had no meaning; her time with Don, the five years she and Ward had been separated—all that disappeared in a gust of the hot wind of passion.

A groan escaped from him and she felt his hips rise to her hand. She was stroking the hot length of his manhood, only the thin material of his briefs between the soft flesh of her fingers and the hard evidence of his need. Suddenly that barrier was more than she could tolerate, and her hand urgently began pulling his jeans below his hips. He shifted to help her, and his jeans and briefs were soon thrown onto the floor.

The startling sight of his magnificent body, a body proud and unashamed of its desire for her, made her stop in admiration for a moment. But Ward's hands didn't pause, and her jeans were soon on the pile with his.

To her surprise, he resumed his position on the sofa and pulled her down on top of him. The back of the sofa once again supported her while she lay half over him, the contact of their bodies instantly driving out all other thoughts but those of Ward and her fundamental need.

Lost in the sensual vortex Ward always created within her, she gave in to the craving to touch him. Her fingers caressed the masculine hardness, drawing a moan of primal pleasure from the depth of his being.

She became aware of a feverish tension growing inside her, fed by the erotic paradox of the velvet steel beneath her stroking hands. His heat was overwhelming her, her blood moving through her limbs like liquid flames.

Ward's hand unerringly remembered her body's most secret, sensitive places, making her quiver with mounting desire. His lips tasted the skin just under her jawline. She felt his tongue steal out between his teeth to leave a moistened trail behind the tiny kisses, kisses that matched the rhythm of his hips as they tensed and thrust upward, his arms encircling her like steel bands.

Near the edge of her consciousness, Stacy heard the ragged gasps of her breath. The tightening coil of desire had every part of her in its grip, demanding fulfillment. Ward must have sensed the change in pitch, for his arm clasped her tighter to him, his other hand cupping a breast and reveling in the feel of her silken flesh against his rough palm.

A moan of pure pleasure flowed out from her depths when he began tantalizing the taut nipple. His hot, moist breath teased her forehead in ever-shortening gasps and he shifted again until their lips met in a kiss of raging need and desire.

His hand left her breast and followed the contours of

her body, its tingling touch exciting her to an even higher pitch, higher than she thought possible without the coil inside her exploding. She felt his fingers trailing through her intimate, feminine curls to sink into the damp softness of her womanhood.

Instantly her body was on a higher plane, using every heated cell to urge her toward the crashing fulfillment she knew Ward's body was so able to bring her.

Neither of them could wait any longer. Ward withdrew his intimate touch to pull her on top of him, his hands gripping her below her waist, his thumbs caressing the slight hollow of her hips as he positioned her over him.

With a deftness born of a searingly vivid memory, he lowered her over his hardened shaft of desire and a cry of delirious pleasure escaped them both when he entered her.

She leaned forward across his chest, her hands on the sheet beside him supporting the weight of her body. The intimate softness of her womanhood welcomed and gripped his masculine length inside her.

She was lost in a sensual maelstrom and didn't care; what was Stacy and what was Ward no longer mattered. Now there was only this one being of flowing, shared energies and passion that moved to the primal rhythm of their joining's metered poetry.

Slowly she moved her hips up and was drawn further into the whirlpool of sensations when she felt him moving inside her. His body rose to meet hers as she lowered her hips once more down the length of his aroused manhood. But even that small measure of control snapped.

Somewhere from far away she heard inarticulate cries of fulfilled pleasure. She was being consumed by a fire that didn't destroy, but whose flames licked farther and farther upward until they metamorphosed into a blazing, shining comet that tore through her veins and nerves and flesh, leaving a sparkling trail of satiation tingling throughout her entire body.

Instinctively she knew that Ward had held back his own release until the full force of her pleasure had been spent. Now a primal sound came from deep within his chest while his firm short thrusts told her he was following her to that celestial plane of flames and light.

A sheen of perspiration covered them both. Stacy remained laying across his chest, their deep gulps of air naturally synchronized. That delightful lethargy that had always filled her after Ward's lovemaking returned after too long an absence, sweet as water after a long thirst.

Sleepily murmuring words of endearment, Ward kissed her neck and held her close. She shifted slightly to one side of him and they fell asleep, their arms and legs intertwined. The contact was reassuring and comforting and Stacy's sleep was more peaceful than it had been in half a decade.

The insistent beeping of a wristwatch alarm woke her the next morning. She blinked the sleep from her eyes and looked around the van's interior without moving from Ward's side. How could the dim predawn light show her nothing out of the ordinary, when she herself had been so fundamentally changed? All of her hard-won reasons for avoiding another relationship had burst in an explosion of glittering fragments of false rationalization.

She had to have time to think—alone. The thought of returning to Zabriskie Point made her realize that his alarm must have been set from when he'd joined her there. No, too many memories of his soul-wrenching kiss would be there. She decided on going to the lookout point above the valley, hoping the remote overlook would allow her to see beyond Death Valley and into her confusing past.

In the middle of the night they had somehow switched places and now she found herself on the outside of the narrow bed. Moving slowly to keep from waking him, she slid sideways out of the bed. Levering herself to stand, she carefully stuffed the extra pillow next to his side. She was thankful the alarm hadn't bothered the slumbering man; his breathing was still shallow and even.

Dressing quickly and silently, she started to leave but hesitated at the back door. She quietly unlatched her purse and, drawing out a pen and her notepad, scribbled a note telling him where she was going and that she didn't regret last night—she had craved it as much as he—but now she needed time to think. Then, leaving the paper on the dinette table, she glanced at his sleeping form and returned to the back door. Taking a deep breath, she turned the knob and was outside in a moment.

The BMW eagerly took to the long climb up to the lookout's parking lot and Stacy almost regretted having to end the relaxing ride. She shivered slightly when the crisp early morning air blew through her hair, still damp from her quick shower. But she locked her helmet to her motorcycle and started out for the hiking path that led to the rocky mountain point jutting out over the salted valley.

It was a longer walk than she'd realized and, though she was in good shape, Stacy was breathing heavily when she finally reached the projecting lookout. Sitting down on a large boulder, she rested a moment and looked out on the glaring white beds of salt that teased the eye into thinking they were small lakes of water instead of salt crystals shimmering in the first rays of the morning sun.

She let herself be dazzled by the scenery around and below her. Her eyes focused on the Panamint Range which formed the western boundary of the valley, but her mind wasn't seeing the ragged dusky peaks. Instead, images from the past filled her mind's eye.

Pushing aside the tendency to condemn Don out of hand, she slowly, thoughtfully, ran through the fading, tarnished memories of their time together. She knew now that he had been in love with his image of her; not Stacy as she was, but Stacy as he thought she was. And it had taken her all of the last three years to even begin to emerge from the guilt that had caused her. Then the sheer foolishness of blaming herself for falling short of his vision had left its own brand of self-denigration.

But Don had been the one who first introduced her to photography and its glorious visual expression of emotions. And it had been photography that had shown her she could trust her emotions again and helped exorcise the pain her late husband had so carelessly caused. No, she couldn't condemn him completely; though he'd caused much of the ache inside her, he'd also given her the means of working it out in her own way.

She couldn't hate him. What had happened between them had certainly been as much her fault as his. She could have prevented the entire fiasco had she not tried to use him to escape her feelings for Ward. That was something she was justified in feeling guilty about, but that feeling, too, was blunting with time. Don Kemble was firmly in the past, where he belonged.

And now, just as all her old wounds were healing and she was finally regaining her lost equilibrium, Ward Fallbrook reentered her life. Granted, five years had mellowed the tumultuous, fiery, demanding Ward who had pulled her into his life by the force of his vitality alone. The fire was still there—last night had proved that. But the rest? No, she had changed too much in the last half-decade to be mesmerized by him again.

Then why was she here instead of calmly fixing breakfast back at her campsite? The thought brought a brief pang of hunger and the beginnings of thirst, but she thrust it away. She had to know what she wanted; could she calmly walk away from this relationship when she went back to Hannah? Did she want to?

Of course! She wouldn't be caught again by that suffocating net of possession. She had thought she'd reached her goal of emotional independence; his showing up had forcefully told her she had not. She'd only reached a plateau—a plateau from which Ward's presence seemed capable of tumbling her back into the chaos her life had been.

But the same presence that threatened her also enticed her. She couldn't deny that Ward excited her blood, her creativity, her very being; and that that very excitement had once terrified her. She remembered it vividly; ultimately she had run away to escape it.

Now she was scared. Would she lose all that she'd tried so hard to gain? Stacy's eyes searched the misty northern end of the valley for answers. Surely others had sought aid from this mystical, demanding land that stripped away all that was not fundamental to existence.

But no answers came to her.

Rocks falling from the trail to the lookout told her she was no longer alone, and when she turned, she was only half-surprised to find that Ward had followed her. For a brief moment the ascending image blurred with another image, five years younger, and Stacy was shocked at the difference. It was something she'd been doing often, looking at the present Ward and seeing the past one, and now she was thrown into confusion.

He smiled and waved at her when he saw her looking at him and Stacy felt an uncomfortable slipping in her defenses. The younger Ward from her past had meshed perfectly with the young woman she'd been then, but she'd changed—just as Ward had changed, she realized with a jolt.

It was time she stopped seeing the Ward she used to know every time she looked at the man walking up the path toward her.

She smiled and waved back. After all, last night she'd only made love to a memory.

CHAPTER SEVEN

Tiny pebbles crunched under his shoes as he approached. "Thought you might want these," he said quietly, dropping a canteen and a plastic bag filled with tan-colored nuts beside her. He sat down on the other side of them.

"Thanks," she said, glancing at him, then returning her gaze to the valley floor. She licked her dry lips.

Out of the corner of her eye she saw him reach toward her. She tensed, but relaxed when his hand closed on the canteen.

"Here, I think you need a sip of this," he said, and unscrewed the cap and held it before her.

Grateful that he had not challenged her for leaving after last night, she took the water and drank deeply. When she would have thanked him, he stopped her.

"Stacy, I want you to know that what happened last night was special to me," he told her. "I don't think it was a casual gesture for either of us, but neither was it a binding, lifelong commitment."

His silver eyes held hers with a steady gaze and she read the sincerity there. He was right; it hadn't been a permanent commitment, but the ardor in his eyes was not at all the look of a man trying to back away from a relationship.

"We can have so much together," he said, "but what

was and is between us is fragile; it needs to be carefully nurtured to maturity. Out on the dunes I remembered about your mother, and how powerfully her life had affected you. My demands on you ignored that once before and broke the thread between us; I won't risk that again."

Stacy smiled. "You make me sound as if I'm made out of porcelain!"

"Oh, you're made out of flesh and blood all right," he said, returning her smile.

His nearness and his smile were acting on her the way they always had, making her all too aware of just how much flesh and blood she really was. The rock beneath her was suddenly much harder than it had been, and she readjusted her position.

Now was the time to tell him to leave, that she didn't want another relationship—at least not for a long time yet. But she couldn't shut him out and she found herself trying to accommodate him.

"I make no promises, Ward, but if you won't push, I won't run." Nervously she dipped her hand into the bag of pistachios and snapped one open. The noise was loud in the quiet of the lookout.

He was silent for a long while, and Stacy began to worry that he wouldn't accept her compromise. Would he try to pressure her into something she didn't want because of last night? She bowed her head for a moment in emotional weariness. God, she was so tired of running!

"I won't press you now," he said, his voice low. "I want your love, Stacy, but I also want your friendship. And I know I won't get either if I start making demands on you." He took another drink from the canteen and offered it to her, adding with a twinkle in his eyes, "Personal demands, that is. I plan on making plenty of professional demands on you—you're a damn fine reporter."

Stacy laughed in relief. But a disturbing image from when she and Ward had worked together at the *Beacon* flashed through her mind, cutting her laughter short. Their being together on assignments had reinforced their mutual attraction to each other, an attraction that had grown to be the terrifying consuming fire she had finally run away from. Despite Ward's assurances, was that beginning all over again?

She shook her head. Damn it—she had to stop this nonsense! She was acting as if her entire life had been like white-water rafting, careening down a river out of control.

But she wasn't like the helpless Pauline in the early film melodramas—she was a grown woman who could make her own decisions. Granted, some of her decisions had been magnificent failures, but they had been hers. From now on she was going to stop reacting to the past and start acting on the future!

After taking a long swig on the canteen, she turned to Ward with a smile.

"I hate to sound like sour grapes, but my expedition to the sand dunes got cut short yesterday." With a graceful arc of her hand, she indicated the deep shadows in the valley floor below them and the thin rim of light on the Panamint Range to the west. "The sun's just rising and the dunes must be beautiful. Would it be too painful for you to return there?"

Ward grinned. "The psychological damage isn't quite that deep," he said. "Besides, who would be there to save you if I didn't go?"

"You save me? Ha! I don't plan on going out there without water or a hat."

"Ungrateful wretch—at least admit it will be easier for you if I carry your camera bag," he said.

She tied a firm knot in the plastic bag of pistachios and stood up. "Hmmm, I don't know if I can trust you with such valuable equipment. Got any experience?"

He grinned again. "You tell me." When she answered with a look of disgust, he went on. "I used to caddy at a golf course when I was a kid, close enough? I don't know what someone who carries a camera bag is called."

Stacy slung the empty canteen over her shoulder and started down the path to her motorcycle. "They're called lackeys," she threw back at him.

He caught up with her and casually draped his arm across her shoulder, pulling her close to his body. She could feel the muscles in his thighs moving against hers and the heat from his side penetrating her arm. But she didn't move away.

"Lackey, huh? I was thinking more along the lines of 'indispensable photographic assistant' or 'vice-president in charge of film, filters, and flash units,' " he said, smiling.

She was still chuckling when they arrived in the parking area. They were in tune with each other, the feeling of camaraderie having grown stronger, and she decided she was glad he'd followed her to the lookout.

Her motorcycle and his van were the only vehicles in the asphalt lot. She turned toward the BMW and he accompanied her, watching her check the latches of the boot that held her camera equipment. When Stacy started to put her helmet on, Ward took it from her and slowly settled it down over her head.

"Would you like to stop and have breakfast first?" he asked.

She shook her head. "No, I want to be sure and get to

the dunes before the sun rises too high and the shadows disappear."

"All right, slave driver, I'll follow you there," he said. Before she could answer he dropped a kiss on her nose and swung her visor down, snapping it into place.

The motorcycle started easily and she began the long winding descent back down out of the eastern range of mountains. Just before she would go around another of the turns, she would glimpse Ward's van in her rearview mirror.

So much had happened since she'd entered the national monument and had seen that same sight. She recalled her trepidation and smiled at it.

Something still felt wrong. What could it be? She distinctly remembered putting the two saddlebags into her tent before she'd left for the lookout and she'd just checked the boot and it was still snug.

But something was missing. Had she dropped something in the parking area? She mentally retraced her steps at the lookout, but when she came to the part when Ward had walked to his van she froze. She recovered immediately and took the next turn with no problems, but she knew what she was missing.

Ward. He wasn't riding with her and she was missing him! She finally reached the straight stretch of road and turned the throttle toward her, speeding northward. By the time she arrived at the sand dunes, she was able to resolutely ignore the revelation.

He arrived shortly after her. They filled the canteen at the tiny sink in the TransVan and, after she'd exchanged her camera's 50 millimeter lens for a 200 millimeter one, they set off. Ward carried the canteen over one shoulder and her camera bag over the other.

Trudging up the first dune, Stacy heard a grunt of exasperation behind her. She turned to see him tilting to one side, struggling with the camera bag strap.

"What have you got in this thing? Concrete blocks?" he complained.

"Just some film, an extra camera body, and two lenses," she told him matter-of-factly. What was he complaining about? She normally carried two additional lenses and a flash unit! "I can carry it if you want me to."

"No, I'll do it, I'll just be three inches shorter on one side, that's all."

The photo session at the sand dunes went smoothly. They began to work in tandem—Ward usually silent, accepting an exposed roll of film and handing Stacy a fresh roll without comment. Occasionally he would quietly mention that a bird had perched on a nearby scraggly branch of one of the low desert bushes that grew on the edge of the dunes.

Stacy would turn to give him a roll of film and find him watching her intently. She wondered at it briefly, but she became absorbed in her work and rarely came out of her "creative fog." Because of that, she felt an exhilarating sense of accomplishment when the session finally ended.

"I got some great shots! I only wish I didn't have to wait until Saturday to develop them!" she said, walking back with Ward to the parking area. Her eyes sparkled with enthusiasm and she smiled up at him.

"Your help did it, Ward. This time I wasn't always fumbling when I needed a fresh roll of film or worrying about packing everything back in properly when I changed a lens. Thanks!"

Her smile widened and she turned her face toward the horizon as if expecting something wonderful to appear.

She was caught up in the pleasure of the photo session and didn't see the tender expression on Ward's face as he watched her.

Lunch was an enjoyable affair and the afternoon photo session at the outdoor museum at Furnace Creek went even better than the morning one. That evening Ward escorted a tired but happy Stacy to her tent.

"Thanks for all your help today," she told him through a yawn. She kept blinking to keep her eyes from closing completely, but her blinks were getting slower and slower.

She felt rather than heard Ward's amused chuckle. It wasn't until his hands grasped her shoulders and pulled her away from him that she realized her head had fallen against his chest. She smiled at him and blinked her eyes. During that long blink she felt his warm, moist lips on her forehead.

He drew his finger down the side of her face to her chin. His head began to descend to hers, but a tender smile lifted the corners of his lips and he shooed her into her tent.

Finally her sleepy body snuggled down into her sleeping bag. Tired but content at the day's work, she let the warmth from Ward's kiss suffuse her body and she fell asleep with a rare smile of happiness on her lips.

"Been to a ghost town lately?" Stacy asked him three days later over breakfast. She was sitting across from Ward on the stone picnic bench at their campsite, and though the scrambled eggs and sausages he'd made were delicious, she was anxious to begin the day's activities.

"Not recently," he answered slowly, giving her a look that said, What are you planning on dragging me into today?

"Great!" she said, ignoring his hesitation. The last few

days had been so productive, she had to try and recapture that creative intensity again. "Rhyolite's just outside the monument boundary in Nevada. It's newer than most ghost towns—early twentieth century instead of late nineteenth—but it has some fantastic buildings that are still partially standing."

"If it's as far away as it sounds, we'd better take the van today," he said.

A light wind had been blowing through their campsite, forcing them to anchor their paper plates and cups. They were protected by the mountain range to the east of them, so the wind didn't bode well for the more open areas beyond.

Stacy frowned but realized it was a good idea. "Okay, but don't forget to get gas in Furnace Creek. There's nothing even remotely resembling a place to stop between here and Rhyolite." At least in the van she wouldn't be continually assaulted by his body being so close to her.

When they were on the road Stacy gave directions from the passenger seat. She watched Ward easily guide the vehicle around the winding turns. His long lithe body sat in the driver's seat like an alert mountain lion, seemingly at rest but able to react instantly.

Just watching the muscles in his arms tense where they were exposed below his rolled-up sleeves made her recall those same arms around her when they'd made love. She mentally shook herself and let her eyes nonchalantly wander to the passing scenery. She'd been glad to avoid his sensuous assault behind her on the motorcycle, but the visual one was proving just as effective.

Her eyes traveled over the sparse vegetation on the mountains around them, but her mind was much further away, and she bit her lip when she recalled her success and

130

enthusiasm of the last few days. Would it be the same today?

There seemed to have been an almost telepathic link between them, a link that gradually evolved from two people working together into one entity of creative energy. That oneness had overcome her; it had been equally seductive to her artistic senses as his body was to her more tangible senses.

The lavender rocks covering the ground announced the town of Rhyolite. Stacy descended quickly and started scouting where she wanted to begin.

Scattered around them were concrete and stone buildings, all in various stages of decomposition. Directly in front of her was the old bank building, with only two of its four walls still standing and intriguing steps leading downward.

"What do you think? Isn't it grand?" she asked Ward when he came up beside her. He had brought her coat and helped her into it, his hands remaining on her shoulders after she'd zipped up the down jacket. The wind was blowing and the higher altitude made it colder than it had been on the valley floor.

"It's not exactly the way I'd pictured it," he said, bending down to speak close to her ear so he could be heard over the wind. "I guess I expected something from a John Wayne movie set, not a town from 1925."

She turned around to face him, purposely breaking the intimate contact. "Thanks for the coat," she began, but a creaking behind her made her spin quickly to her former position. Seeing an iron railing barely hanging on to a second-story window of the bank, she said, "I have to get a picture of that! It's perfect."

Walking to the van to get her camera bag, she shouted

back to him, "The Wild West lasted longer than most people think, especially in isolated towns like this one."

Once she began shooting again, the creative fog descended rapidly. Ward was always near her, though she was mostly unaware of it and that part of her that was aware of it considered him to somehow be an extension of herself.

It was nearing noon when, after a particularly long session, she turned with the camera still to her eye to take a picture of Ward. Looking through the viewfinder, she felt a moment of disorientation. He was sitting on a low wall in the exact position as he had in the picture she'd saved from the trash can back in Hannah. Like a time-warped double exposure, Stacy wavered between the girl she was when she'd taken that first picture and the woman she was now, watching him in Rhyolite.

She shook her head and the differences in the two pictures became more apparent. The camera bag sitting between his feet, the scraggly bushes behind him instead of the lush verdure of the park, and even his expression was different.

In the earlier picture he had watched her with tenderness and a touch of indulgence. But now his look was much more openly admiring, the tenderness was still there —mixed with respect this time—and his desire for her was blatant but controlled. In that instant she realized that while he was giving her room, he certainly wasn't giving up.

They had lunch in the van and then returned to Death Valley, Stacy taking photographs of several more sights. After the exhausting afternoon they returned to their campsite that evening hungry and tired.

"Why don't we eat in the van tonight? It's not too

chilly, but this wind's going to make it difficult to eat outside," Ward said, struggling with the newspaper he'd picked up at the Furnace Creek Inn on their way back.

"Whatever you say," Stacy said with a yawn. A tingling sense of being gloriously alive was woven through her tiredness.

She set her camera equipment inside her tent and stood up in front of the nylon hemisphere, stretching hard to work the kinks out of her muscles. A smile played over her lips, changing intensity with memories of the day going through her mind.

Fortunately Ward volunteered to fix dinner that night. Stacy was so tired, she didn't think she'd know a can of peas from a jar of peanut butter.

"Hmmm?" Stacy could remember that Ward had asked her a question, but she couldn't remember what it was. She opened her eyes and saw him sitting across the van's small dining table from her, a gentle smile on his face.

Her left elbow was on the table, her hand supporting her head since it was much too heavy for her neck to hold up by itself. The way Ward was sprawled on the seat cushions told her he was as tired as she was.

"Cm'on, let's get you to bed," he sighed, standing with an effort.

His arm came down to encircle her shoulders and she felt herself lean into the hard chest bending toward her. When he opened the door to the van and the cooler night wind buffeted against them, she snuggled even further into his embrace.

The night air revived them slightly, but they were both already half asleep and they relied on each other for support. When they reached her tent, Stacy put out a hand and held the zipper tab while Ward unzipped the door opening. Once open, she started to bend forward to enter and stumbled over the slightly raised flap at the bottom of the door. It was supposed to keep out dirt and mud, but at the moment it seemed intent on keeping her out.

Ward kneeled down and crawled inside, then turned and helped her enter. It was dark in the small nylon dome, but once out of the wind, it was also much warmer.

Unthinkingly Stacy zipped up the door again and started to lay down on top of her sleeping bag, too tired to get inside. Her knee caught on the edge of the thin closed-cell foam mattress and she would have fallen forward had his arms not immediately gone around her.

With instinct rather than thought governing her actions, she let him slowly lower her to the sleeping bag. They lay, spoon-fashion, and a minute of contentment passed, then two, and she only snuggled further into the warmth of his body curving around hers.

Somewhere in that limbo between waking and sleeping, she felt a spark of delicious fire on her neck. She murmured and felt another spark, then another and another, tracing the hairline at her neck to her ear. When hot breath made the sensitive nerves under her skin dance and the warmth of porcelain teeth teased her delicate lobe, she couldn't restrain her body's responses.

"Mmm," she moaned. Her conscious mind had already begun to give itself up to sleep and her body gloried in its delight. The nibbles at her ear were wreaking their own kind of disaster on her blood and she slowly turned toward him, her eyes half-closed with sleep and desire.

His lips, which had claimed her ear, now claimed her mouth. It was a soft kiss, a slow kiss that rippled across the sensitive skin of her lips with a languid, burning heat.

She could feel his tongue tasting the rose-colored flesh, stroking the edges of her lips.

Tingling, tightening desire was caressing the lower part of her body like the white froth of a wave on a gently sloping beach. But though it lacked the crashing thunder of the pounding surf, she knew that passion would rise within her as inexorably as the tide.

She found herself giving in to it. Ward's hands reveled in the silken skin of her arms beneath the rustling material of her down jacket. But it was warm, so wonderfully warm, and when he removed their jackets, she didn't protest.

His fingers traced her collarbone, the light touch electric on her skin. In response she pressed him closer and her hands felt the firm muscles in his lower back tense when their hips met. The action fed her need to feel the texture of his flesh beneath her hands, and she languorously pulled his shirt from the waistband of his jeans.

The rough flesh of his fingertips caressed her skin above the open V of her blouse. With each twist of his fingers to free another button, he kissed her just where the pinkness was newly exposed.

His lips descended with the opening blouse and when the material was completely unfastened, his kisses explored the tantalizing niche of her navel. She writhed in growing need when his tongue licked the very edge of that small indentation and teased the tiny strands of red-gold hair swirling there.

Then his kisses ascended once more to outline the high firm mounds of her breasts. Responding to the current arcing through her each time his lips feathered the creaminess of her skin, she arched her back toward him.

Her own fingers had found the buttons of his shirt and

135

released them, opening up the expanse of his muscled chest to her questing touch. While one hand was buried deep in his mass of thick dark curls, the other reveled in the feel of his taut velvet skin.

At last his mouth reached the peak of her waiting breast and she cried out in a breathy crescendo of passion. Each spark flashed through her directly to the core of her womanhood, striking the banked fires into flames of passion. He sucked the flushed nipple between his teeth and his tongue teased the hardening tip till she cried out.

"I want you! I need you, Ward, how I need you," she breathed in her delirium not even knowing what she was saying. For days they had been so emotionally close that at times she had felt them to be almost one. Now her body was crying out for that ultimate union which would indeed make them one.

"Ah, sweet Stacy, I'm here," he murmured, kissing the line of her jaw between each word while his hand stroked the satin skin of her side. "My love . . . my love . . . my life." Their mouths met in a kiss that drew her into him, their lips pressing together and their tongues intertwining in wordless communication of their desire.

Her hands struggled with the fastenings of his jeans as he undid hers. She drew the soft denim over his hips, her hands caressing the hair-rough skin of his thighs until he moved slightly and cast them off completely. Her own jeans soon followed.

She craved to have his body covering hers, but he withheld that final moment to trace at her outline of her body in the darkness of the tent. His head lowered and his lips kissed along her hipbone, the soft curls of his hair caressing her flat stomach.

The moist warmth of his mouth traveled even farther to

the warmth flesh of her inner thighs and she ached for release. His hands slid up and down the backs of her legs while he kissed the smooth skin. Her head turned from side to side as the kisses so close to her womanhood spun a web of intense longing around her very soul.

She could feel his tongue darting between his lips to taste her, as if letting no sense escape him. His kisses led upward, and she thought he could not take her higher than he already had, but when his loving caresses finally reached that most intimate place, her breathing became even more ragged with her cries of desire.

Suddenly his body was over hers and she moaned with anticipation. His thighs were on her thighs and his chest on hers. She unconsciously reached for the mounds of his buttocks and felt them tense as he lowered his hips toward hers. In the space of a heartbeat they were united into one entity and their perfect union was complete.

They moved to a single rhythm, each matching the other's movements. A slow steady pulse of liquid fire beat through her veins. Ward's thrusts increased and the pulse of fire quickened within her.

She distantly heard inarticulate moans of passion but did not recognize their source. Her entire consciousness was focused on their lovemaking. Her hands tightened their grip on him as she pulled him to her in the same instant that all her longings were satisfied and the web dissolved into liquid heat. Every nerve in her body cried out with its pleasure.

She felt his body tense over hers and he followed her with his own volcanic release, a primal groan escaping from deep within his chest.

He lay over her until their breathing had regained its

evenness. His breath stirred the damp hair near her ear and she smiled and impulsively kissed his cheek.

She felt rather than saw his smile and he tenderly kissed her where her neck sloped to her shoulder. They talked of private inconsequential things, their gentle laughter frequently interrupted by a kiss. But the heat from their lovemaking was dissipating and Stacy shivered. Their bodies were covered in a slight sheen of perspiration which the night air quickly chilled.

He kissed her eyelids and asked, "Can we both fit in this thing?"

"We could, but you have to promise not to steal the covers—you'd also be stealing the whole bed!"

They settled into the sleeping bag, Stacy half on top of Ward, but he didn't seem to mind and she certainly didn't. Her head fit perfectly into the hollow of his shoulder and, with his arm around her, she drifted asleep. A glow of happiness suffused her, but it was a happiness she did not risk putting into words.

CHAPTER EIGHT

She woke at dawn, tense and covered with perspiration. An uneasiness had settled over her and she shook her head to dispel the unwanted fragments of disturbing dreams. At first her dreams had been vague images of contentment, but then those visions had become those of suffocating confinement.

Their positions had not changed during the night and her movements woke the man beside her. He kissed her hair and hugged her to him. "Mornin', honey," he said, his voice still drowsy with sleep.

"Good morning," she said, "sleep well?"

He murmured his assent and she felt the reverberations in his chest. "You?"

She nodded, feeling the smooth taut muscles of his shoulder move under the side of her face pressed into him. But she hadn't slept well; her dreams had disturbed her more than she wanted to admit. What had happened to the elation and rapture of the night before?

Rising and dressing, she tried to shake off the uneasiness, but when she met Ward again at the stone table, it had not diminished.

"I hate to see this day begin," he told her, handing her a cup of coffee and preparing to fix a hearty breakfast.

"You don't have to go to all this trouble, Ward," she told him, not sure why she was protesting the delicious food, "a roll would have been fine."

"Oh, I know you artist types," he said, smiling. "You'd forget to eat altogether if someone wasn't there reminding you. Remember yesterday at Rhyolite? I finally had to withhold your film to get you inside the van to have some lunch!"

She grinned back, but something inside squirmed at his words. She wasn't as absentminded as he'd made her sound. Did he really think her so incapable?

Remembering his earlier comment, she asked, "What's wrong with today? The wind's died down and the temperature's perfect."

"Hannah is what's wrong," he said. "In case you've forgotten, it's Friday and we have to be back for Roberts's retirement party on Saturday night, unless you were planning on missing it."

"Of course I'm not going to miss it! I was going to leave around seven tonight to play it safe. I couldn't take another ride like the one coming out here."

They decided to visit Stovepipe Wells and Ward insisted on driving the van. Stacy tried to convince him that it would be no problem to take the BMW, but he gently overrode her protests.

"Here, let me take that for you," Ward offered, slipping her camera bag off her shoulder.

"No, I wanted to—" she began, but he'd already begun packing it snugly in a cupboard under the sofa.

Her gaze lifted from his hand closing the brass-colored latch to the sofa. The unrumpled sheets reminded her of the night before and her unwelcome dreams. She shivered.

Was her body making commitments for her that she did not want to make?

The day deteriorated rapidly and by late afternoon she was in a foul mood. He had not failed to anticipate her needs—not once! His telepathic senses were unnerving her, making her realize just how close they had become in a week's time.

Somehow she had to let him know that what had happened here in Death Valley was an isolated incident. She shouldn't have let the relationship go as far as it had, but it certainly wasn't going to go any further. But she knew he would not accept that decision readily.

He nosed the van into the campsite and Stacy sighed in relief. The day—and week—was almost over! She could return to Hannah and her normal life.

She opened the van's door immediately and started to descend, but his hand closed around her arm.

"Ward," she said, an unmistakable note of warning in her voice.

"You don't have to be in quite so big a hurry, do you?" he asked. She didn't like his low, menacing tone, but she answered him as calmly as she could.

"It's almost six now," she said, "and I told you I needed to leave by seven."

He stood between the seats, his tall frame leaning over her. "Surely one more minute won't make that much difference." He'd obviously sensed that she was backing away from him, rebuilding the barriers.

His face was inches from hers and she could see the hard, uncompromising gleam in the gray gaze that raked her. "I told you I won't let you run away again, and I meant it. After yesterday and last night," he said, shaking his head, "no, I'm not going to let you give that up."

His features swam before her eyes for an instant, then his mouth covered hers in a kiss that reinforced his possessive words. The force of that assault broke through her resistance and plundered her inner secrets. She wanted to fight him, to struggle to gain the upper hand, but she couldn't. It was too difficult to fight her own inner battle of her unwanted responses to him.

The soft, insistent steel of his lips slid over her pliant ones; she could deny his questing tongue nothing. But she kept her hands at her sides, though they ached to caress the muscles at the base of his neck. She might not be able to prevent her body from responding to him, but she would try her damnedest to keep Ward from knowing the depth of that reaction.

He broke the kiss and his eyes scanned her face, the gray gaze a puzzling mixture of challenge, bracing himself for her reaction.

Shaken, she remained silent for a moment to regain her equilibrium. She tried to act as she would have if he hadn't kissed her. It was difficult to keep her body still and she was unable to prevent her voice from quivering.

"I'll see you tomorrow night at Robbie's retirement party," she said. She left the van and began to pack her things, starting with her clothes and sleeping bag and ending with her tent.

Struggling with the tent stakes, she looked up to see Ward standing near his van watching her. When their eyes met, he started toward her, but she deliberately let her eyes drift away and resumed her task, ignoring him completely. He did not offer to help.

The ride home was long but uneventful. Her eyes kept glancing to the rearview mirror, though she refused to think about her reasons for doing so. But the distinctive lights of his TransVan never appeared.

"Stacy! You're back just in time to say good-bye," Robbie told her, giving her a bear hug. She was in the center of the group of reporters from the *Monitor*. Someone had decided that the banquet room at the Holiday Inn ten miles out of town on Highway 99 was the perfect spot for a retirement party. Consequently Stacy's ride had been long and cold, since the weather had turned bad.

"I'll miss you, Robbie," she said, returning his hug. That was truer than she wanted it to be, and with low spirits she tightened her hold for an instant before stepping back from the older man.

He sensed her mood and said in a subdued voice only she could hear, "Are you feeling all right? It's too cold for that motorcycle of yours. I'm pleased as punch that you came tonight, but I don't want you getting sick on account of me."

"No, I'm fine, Robbie," she said, "just sad to see you go, that's all."

"Not too sad, I hope—I'll still be around, and this Fallbrook seems like an excellent fellow. And you've worked with him before—" Roberts was interrupted then by someone from the circle of well-wishers.

"You sure you won't get bored doing nothing but fishing? Sounds dull to me," Clancy's voice said.

"Fishing? Dull? My dear boy, that's impossible. Besides, I've signed on with Sierra Fishing Tours to lead some of their 'advanced' groups—should be fun," the editor said, smiling at the people gathered around him.

Stacy managed to merge into the general gathering and quickly found herself on the outside edge of the party. But she discovered soon enough that that was a bad place to be if one wanted to avoid confidences.

The night editor, Melody Atkins, sidled up to her, saying, "Everybody's wondering about Fallbrook—can you imagine what it's going to be like to work for someone who looks like that? I hope he works late—really late!" Stacy tried her best to return Melody's you-know-what-I'm-talking-about smile, but it was difficult when she felt so miserable.

She'd come to the party hoping to forget that beginning Monday morning she'd be working with Ward on a daily basis. But naturally at Robbie's going away party everyone was curious—and talkative—about how things were going to be.

Elly came up beside her. "How was your vacation? We missed you at the *Monitor,*" the woman said. "Don't you get lonely on those solitary trips of yours?"

Stacy started to speak, but the doors opened on the far side of the room and Ward entered. His eyes scanned the room, coming to rest on her for a moment before continuing on. "I—ah, no, no, I don't get lonely. Sometimes just the opposite, in fact," Stacy finally answered. She was sure Elly had seen that peculiar look Ward had given her—a look that said he was going to corner her sooner or later.

"Are you sure you're okay? You look kind of peaked," Elly said, leading her to one of the chairs lining the wall. "I'm sure Robbie wouldn't mind if you had to go home early."

Stacy forced a laugh and was surprised at how genuine it sounded. "No, I'm fine, really! Just a bit tired. I only need a day or two to recuperate from my vacation! My trips are supposed to be relaxing, but they usually end up utterly exhausting."

144

That answer seemed to work throughout the rest of the evening as she mingled with the staff of the *Monitor* and their spouses and companions. She ended up hearing about exhausting trips to three-fourths of the known universe, including the popcorn capital of the world somewhere in Tennessee, but it was worth it since no one seemed to notice that her mingling kept taking her farther away from Ward Fallbrook.

Finally the fete was over and Stacy gratefully made for the exit, her jacket clutched in one hand and her purse in the other. She only stopped near the door to put on her coat.

"It won't be this easy in the newsroom," Ward whispered.

She jumped in surprise and turned to face him, her coat dangling from one arm. Evidently her actions hadn't escaped everyone's notice.

"You can't threaten me with that and you know it," she said with a determined glint in her eyes. The evening's success had given her courage that she might otherwise have lacked. "You're caught in your own ethics. You would never be less than professional in the newsroom—casual, yes, but never unprofessional."

She turned to go, but he had grasped the empty sleeve of her coat and prevented her from leaving. But to keep the action looking as normal as possible, he grinned and bowed gracefully and assisted her into the rest of her jacket.

"You may be right, my love," he said, keeping his voice low so only she could hear. "But then you do odd things to my senses—who knows what I may do?" He smiled and stepped back. "See you Monday—seven sharp!"

* * *

145

She walked into the newsroom on Monday and immediately felt Ward's presence. He was easily on top of all the reporter's stories, his questions cogent and to the point. The air was subtly charged with enthusiasm in a way it had never been with Robbie sitting at the editor's desk.

At lunch she heard his praises sung all around her—he obviously meant them all to work harder, dig deeper, and write clearer. And they loved it.

The first few days were relatively easy. Ward was busy learning all there was to know about the ins and outs of Hannah. The paper didn't cover a big area, but it was an important one where events could affect many lives. She even found herself partially caught up in the new vitality, but she still couldn't forget who was assigning the stories.

Though she thought he stood closer to her than necessary when asking a question, or let his eyes wander over her more than normal, she began to relax. Maybe that last threat after Robbie's retirement party had just been his ego talking—not wanting her to have the last word.

She usually loved Friday nights. Most people did, but for her they were really special. Not only did she not have a single meeting to go to, but she could stay up as late as she wanted working in her darkroom.

But now she was having a tough time explaining that to the man standing on her doorstep.

"It's Friday evening, Ward, and there's not a council meeting in sight. I'm staying at home."

"Fine," he said, shouldering his way past her into the hallway. "I'll stay with you."

"Ward! Damn it, I'm working in my darkroom," she said, following him into her kitchen.

"Look's like you're standing in the kitchen to me."

146

"Don't be an ass—you know what I mean," she said. But puzzlement replaced her anger as she watched him look through her cupboards.

"Don't you have a wok?" he asked, as if she hadn't spoken. But before she could answer, he dragged out a large frying pan and said, "This'll do."

"Ward, what are you doing?"

"Fixing dinner." He rummaged through her refrigerator, throwing various items that caught his eye out on the counter.

"I knew I shouldn't have answered the doorbell," she muttered.

"Go on up to your darkroom; I'll call you when it's ready," he said, shooing her up the stairs. She wanted to protest, but half of her mind was already in the small room upstairs and she went without further complaints.

During the past week she'd been able to develop the rolls of film she'd taken at Death Valley. She hummed while mixing up a fresh batch of chemicals, then coughed as she poured the ammonia-based fix into the distilled water.

That done, she carefully washed off the utensils in the stainless steel sink. She grinned, remembering the pile of unfiled proof sheets waiting on her desk; after tonight, there'd be an even larger stack of them to file.

A knock came on her door and a plastic beaker fell from her grasp to the floor. The door opened and Ward came in, but before he could say anything, she turned on him.

"Don't you ever open that door again without my telling you it's okay! What if I'd been opening a box of photo paper? God knows how much you could have ruined!" Her voice was low, which was more threatening than if she had shouted.

147

"Aren't you overreacting?" he asked quietly.

Stacy barely heard his words through the fog of anger in her mind. "No, I am not! You barge into my house, take over my kitchen, and then blithely walk into my darkroom without waiting for me to tell you it's okay! You're damn lucky I haven't thrown a film tank at you. I think you've outstayed what little welcome you had."

"I had no welcome at all, if you'll think back."

"Why did you come over then? I was perfectly happy this past week," she said, pushing away the memories of her sleepless nights.

"You know I didn't have a minute to myself this week, or I'd've been here sooner," he said, watching her with narrowed eyes and his hands thrust into his pockets. "I gave up too soon when you went to Don; now I'm not going to give up at all."

"Ward . . ." A thread of panic wound through her.

"No, Stacy, not after what happened in Death Valley."

"Leave me alone," she whispered.

"And ruin both our lives? No, I won't do that—not again."

He had remained standing near the door, but she could feel his presence in every part of her being. But she denied it;—she had to deny it. She remembered her father's suffering and Don's spite, knowing that if Ward ever felt that way about her, she would not survive it.

"You're too big to throw out," she said. "Do what you want; I won't be paying attention anyway."

She walked passed him and went to the kitchen, knowing he would follow her. They ate in silence; the cold stir-fried chicken and vegetables was the most unpalatable mess she'd ever tried to eat.

* * *

For several weeks Ward was as businesslike as she could have wished in the newsroom. But every night she was free, he would stop by and sit in her darkroom, watching her while she developed prints from the film she'd shot while in Death Valley.

"Why don't you let me do that?" Ward asked, seeing her slip an exposed print into the developer.

"Are you sure you want to? Rocking a developer tray isn't the most exciting part of photography," Stacy told him. She hadn't noticed that during his frequent visits the tense atmosphere had eroded into a pleasant sort of companionship, though both were unconsciously careful not to overstep the bounds of that friendliness.

The timer beeped and she picked up the print with her tongs and slipped it into the stop bath. A faint sizzling sound accompanied the chemical's action of preventing the developer from going further.

"This part seems simple enough." He straightened from leaning against the stainless steel sink that ran along one wall. "It's that part that's beyond me," he said, pointing to the enlarger on the opposite side of the small room.

He stood next to her, and every nerve ending tingled with his closeness. He hadn't tried to kiss her again since the kiss in his van at Death Valley, but her body remembered the exquisite sensations he could create.

The timer beeped again and brought her attention back to the trays of chemicals lined up in the sink. "All right, let's see how long you can last without getting bored. Here are the tongs—you grip the edge of the print to put it into the fix or whatever, but then you just lift a corner of the tray to gently agitate the liquid so fresh solution is always next to the print," she said, performing the task as she explained it. "Got that?"

He nodded. "What about the timer? Is this the reset button?" He gestured to his left, but he was reaching around her to lift the corner of the fix tray as she'd shown him.

Her breathing became erratic when she suddenly found herself nestled against his chest. How had it happened? But though she half-anticipated his kiss, he didn't even try it, and she could hardly complain when he was occupied with a mundane task for her.

"Right," she said, maneuvering herself away from him. "It's already programed for the proper time limit for each step, so all you have to do is press Reset when the print's put into the developer."

He smiled at her and nodded. She returned his smile, but lowered her eyes and quickly turned back to the enlarger. How could she have known how compelling gray eyes would be under the soft golden glow of the amber safe light?

She glanced behind her at the masculine frame inches from her own. He had rested his left hand against the edge of the sink while he leaned over to look at the picture in the tray.

She took the negative carrier out of the enlarger and slid the strip of negatives to the next frame. Replacing the carrier, she flipped on the focus light and, turning the knob on the side of the enlarger, brought the picture into focus.

It was the picture of Ward she'd taken at Rhyolite, the picture so like the one tacked to the wall above her desk. She had to stifle an exclamation of annoyance and was half-tempted to yank the negative out and put in another one. Why must everything remind her of the man standing so close behind her?

But as she reached for the carrier to remove the negative, the processing timer went off.

"What do I do now?" Ward asked, holding the paper by the corner and letting it drip into the tray.

"Put it into that washing tray at the end of the sink," she said, indicating a clear acrylic box overflowing with water. "Thanks. I'll have a test strip ready in a minute."

For a moment she was afraid he was going to turn and watch over her shoulder as she made the next print. A silent sigh of relief escaped her when she saw him lean against the sink to wait for the next print.

She quickly made the necessary test strip and handed it to him. Not being able to do anything until she got the results from the strip, she watched him.

He had characteristically rolled his shirt-sleeves up to just below his elbow, and her gaze followed the muscles in his arms tensing and relaxing as he rocked the developer tray. When the timer went off, he carefully lifted the test strip and placed it in the stop bath. He gently arranged the sizzling paper in the acetic acid solution.

Stacy lifted her eyes to his face and saw the concentration there. It was a simple task for him, yet he brought to it a kind of respect. With a start she realized that that was one of the things she loved—liked—about him most. That jobs most people would do carelessly because they were simple or menial, Ward would do well.

Everything to him was worth doing well, even a relationship. He would never subject her to cutting jibes as Don had. Her mind drifted and she found herself imagining what life with Ward would be like.

No! To judge by his actions, she'd finally managed to convince him that his friendship was acceptable but that

151

any other idea was impossible. She rubbed her forehead to clear it of an unwelcome sadness.

"The fumes getting to you?" Ward asked. "I don't see how you can do this night after night."

"What an idiot I am! I forgot to turn on the fan," she said. She reached for a switch and a droning whir started up.

The test strip was done, but she had to make several prints of the picture of Ward before she had it exactly the way she wanted it. She didn't know why, but her usually critical eye was an even harsher critic with that print. Either the sky was too light or the shadows too dense and showed no detail. Something in her mind had decreed that this print had to be perfect and, finally, she thought she'd done it.

Ward was pulling the final, perfect, print from the fix when a staccato sound invaded their concentration. Stacy looked toward the fan on the wall, where the sound was coming from.

"Guess we're in for some rain."

The rain continued for three days and there was no letup in sight. The first day, Stacy had pulled into her garage damp and cold and miserable under the raingear she wore.

Ward arrived early the next morning and she didn't protest much when he insisted she ride to work with him. He handed her an extra set of keys so she could drive the Saab to assignments, but she refused until he reminded her that if she didn't take them, he'd give them to her in front of the entire newsroom. She took them.

But she didn't have to use his car much. The reporters

152

relied heavily on telephones to get their stories, but by the third day, the rain was the story.

The police scanner was droning on Clancy's desk while she finished a story. The red-haired reporter sitting at the desk in front of hers stiffened and turned up the volume on the scanner. Stacy quickly filed her piece and listened.

Clancy swiveled in his chair and turned toward Ward at the back of the room. "They're evacuating Jondaw Valley below the reservoir."

"That's my beat," Stacy said, rising from her chair and grabbing her purse and reporter's notebook at the same time.

Ward glanced at the clock on the wall and then frowned at her. The lights flickered and several curses went up when the terminals blanked out. Fortunately Ward had told everyone to file their stories often for just that reason, and only a few paragraphs were lost.

But a worried frown still creased Ward's forehead. "Stacy, it's too near deadline. If the electricity goes completely, we'll have only just enough emergency power to get the paper out. Call the sheriff's office and find out what you can. We'll print a bulletin in today's edition."

She didn't agree but knew better than to argue. Sitting back down, she called the sheriff and learned that the reservoir was well over its capacity and had developed cracks from the pressure of the water.

When all the stories were in and the paper was almost ready to hit the presses, Ward rose to go to Production to check the paste-ups. He motioned Stacy to follow him.

In the corridor outside of the production room, he gripped her shoulders. "You be careful, damn it. We don't need Pulitzer prize stuff, just get the story without endangering yourself. And don't worry about the car—it'll get you out of most spots you can drive into."

He looked at her intently and she thought for a moment that he was going to kiss her. But he dropped his burning grip and walked into Production without another word.

The windshield wipers were swacking rapidly back and forth in a hopeless attempt to clear away the sheets of water. Stacy was gripping the wheel with white-knuckled hands as she leaned forward to peer out into the distorted world beyond the car.

But while she concentrated on the road she couldn't prevent Ward's face from intruding into the back of her mind. Why had he looked at her so fiercely? The man who had walked into the production room was a far cry from the man who'd been in her darkroom three days before.

She neared her turn and had to slow to a crawl to be sure she didn't miss the corner. Through the dim grayness that seemed to be all that was left of the world, she spotted the street sign, then panicked for a moment when she couldn't remember if the sign was on the near or far side of the road. She slowed the car down even more.

The rain let up briefly and another car's lights coming up the side road solved her problem. She turned onto the road and, as the car passed her, the tarpaulin flew up and she saw a television set perched precariously on its roof on top of other household belongings. She encountered the police barricade only a mile further on.

Flashing her press pass, she drove on toward the reservoir. The sheriff at the barricade had warned her not to take too long—the cracks appeared to be worsening and they couldn't be responsible for her.

The parking area was level with the top of the water, but Stacy felt it wiser to park the car well back from the danger area. She grabbed her poncho and the waterproof camera she'd borrowed from the sports editor and started taking pictures.

The reservoir had been built many years ago against a natural curve in the high walls of the valley. Even without the cracks there was a danger of the earthworks of the reservoir overflowing. The whitecaps lapping against the edge would make a fantastic shot, and Stacy slung the camera strap over her neck. She started climbing up the nearby cliff, resolutely putting Ward's warning from her mind.

Fifteen minutes later that warning came forcefully back to her. A large muddy section of the cliff was starting to slide down and it threatened to take her with it. She got back down to the parking lot just in time to see the stream of mud flow across the only exit.

Disgusted at her own stupidity, she pounded on the car's roof in frustration. At least she could sit in the car out of the rain—but Ward was going to be furious when she finally returned to the *Monitor*.

"Well, I did get the pictures I wanted despite that crack about Pulitzer prize stuff," she told the steering wheel. She tried to thrust the image of Ward's face just before he'd gone into Production from her mind.

Resting her head against the wheel, she finally gave up and let herself think of him. He'd been intruding into her thoughts constantly and she knew why. During the last few weeks she'd changed; the time she spent in the darkroom was becoming increasingly important to her.

Was that because Ward was there? No, the importance of her photography was real enough. But a more fundamental change had happened—a new Stacy was emerging, a Stacy who was no longer hiding from herself. A Stacy

155

who could admit that she was in love with Ward Fallbrook and had been for five and a half years.

Could she tell Ward that? That would be the true test of her newfound courage. Then a shiver went through her. She'd insisted that he not press her for a relationship, and to her surprise—especially after the threat at Death Valley —he'd done so. Had he fallen out of love with her? Was friendship all he had to offer her now?

She lifted her head from the steering wheel and looked up at the cliff. It was still oozing mud down into the parking lot, and several dead tree trunks had been caught and were being carried down with the mud. If she didn't get out soon, and the reservoir broke, all her questions would be moot.

Ward had said the car could get her out of almost any place she could drive into. She didn't think this was what he'd had in mind, but she certainly wasn't going to get out by sitting here. Taking a deep breath, she put on her seat belt and reached down between the seats to start the car. It hummed to life.

She remembered one of the cautions her father had told her: if you get in mud, don't let up on the gas until you're through.

Putting the car into first gear, she slowly let out the clutch and aimed it toward the exit. She heard the mud on the underside of the car, but she kept her foot steady on the accelerator throughout the bumpy ride.

Her back tires spun when she was almost free of the sticky ooze and, with a surge of panic at getting stuck, her foot pressed on the gas. She didn't know if it was the best thing she could have done in the front-wheel drive car, but she did know it worked. She was on her way back to the *Monitor*—and Ward.

CHAPTER NINE

"Where the hell have you been?"

"Ward, I . . ."

"Damn it, woman, I told you not to do anything dangerous, and when I called the sheriff I was told you had driven right down to the reservoir!" He was standing inches from her, hovering over her tired frame as if waiting for her to flee.

The newsroom was quiet, Ward's outburst having silenced Clancy and the other reporters. Stacy saw Elly abruptly end a telephone conversation and hang up the receiver quietly; even Elly was afraid to make any noise.

The scene was embarrassing, but Ward seemed unaware of everyone but her. Stacy tried to treat it matter-of-factly, and awkwardly rewound the film in the unfamiliar camera, but the task was made more difficult by her shaking hands.

"Why are you so upset? I was only stuck for an hour or so . . ."

"You left at twelve; it's four now."

She glared at him, her own anger replacing the embarrassment. "Then I'd better get out to the high school gym and interview the 'refugees,' hadn't I?"

"Clancy's going," he said, to that reporter's obvious

surprise. But the young man scrambled out with a look of relief on his face; Ward Fallbrook in a rage was not a comfortable sight.

Clancy's look must have penetrated Ward's anger-fogged brain, for he took a step back from Stacy and jerked his head toward his office door. Her anger had focused on Ward, and she didn't see the carefully blank faces of the others in the newsroom when she followed him. The click of the door behind her signaled that round two was about to begin.

"Was that little spectacle really necessary?" She sat down in a chair in front of his desk, crossing her arms and legs. Her green-gold eyes were shooting sparks.

"You could've been killed!" He sat in the large chair behind his desk and Stacy was disgusted to think he needed to put the large slab of oak between them.

"But I wasn't," she said. She uncrossed her arms and leaned forward. "I had to get some shots of the earth-works. It's the nature of a reporter's job to take some risks—you know that."

"Not ones that might be fatal," he said. "Your life is worth more than any story! I won't let you put yourself in a situation like that again. I'm reassigning you to cover Hannah itself; Clancy can take the southern area you've been covering."

"What! It's okay for Clancy to take risks, and not me? I'm supposed to stay where it's safe and protected, is that it? Come on, Ward." She was pacing now, her agitation too great for her to remain still. A rising feeling of suffocation was filling her and any thought of reconciling with him had vanished.

He was trying to exert a power over her that was other than that of a boss over an employee; even the friendship

158

their relationship had settled into didn't permit him to direct her life this way. It was her life with Don all over again.

"Look, this isn't working out," she said, dropping back down into the chair. "Maybe I ought to—"

"To what? Leave?" he said. His chair squeaked when he leaned forward, his hands splayed on the desktop and his eyes boring into her. His voice lowered to a silken challenge. "Running again, Stacy?"

She stared at the books on the shelf behind him. Without looking at him, she said, "Don't reassign me, Ward."

"Try to get your stories less dangerously," he said.

Her eyes remained on the books, but she nodded.

"Okay, you're still covering the southern end."

She left the room and went and sat in front of her computer terminal but didn't turn it on. When Ward didn't come out of his office after an hour, she asked Elly to take her home.

After a relaxing hot shower and a light dinner she walked up the stairs with heavy feet to her workroom. She wanted to mount some of the prints she'd been making in the darkroom for the past week and tonight would be a good time for that. Tired, but not sleepy, she turned on her dry mount press and dug out the package of mounting tissue along with the tacking iron. The doorbell rang when she was sorting through the mat board.

"If that's Ward, I'm going to shut the door in his face," she muttered, and seriously considered not answering the door at all. But she gave in to the insistent chime and went downstairs.

She stood in the doorway, one hand on her hip and the other holding on to the doorjamb to block the way. "No, you're not coming in, Ward," she said. "You said enough at the *Monitor* this afternoon."

"I came to apologize for overreacting," he said. She could hear the rattle of his keys as he flipped them over and over in the palm of his hand.

"Apology accepted," she said, but her eyes told him otherwise and she didn't move to let him in.

"Let me in, Stacy."

"I'll see you tomorrow. Ward! Put me down!" she cried, her hands automatically going to his shoulders to balance herself while his hands encircled her waist, holding her several inches off the ground. "Put me down! I don't want you in my house."

Ignoring the latter half of her protest, he set her down at the foot of the stairs and kicked the door shut. His hands remained solidly around her waist.

"Now that you've done your Viking-warrior imitation, you can let me go," she spat, "or do I get clubbed and dragged up the stairs by my hair next."

"That first part's tempting," he said. "Stop being so stubborn; I did overdo it this afternoon and I'm sorry."

His fingertips were lightly pressing into her, their warmth burning her through the thin fabric of her blouse, and she stepped onto the first stair to break away from his grasp.

"I told you I accepted your apology." She frowned when she saw he was preparing to follow her upstairs. "There's no need for you to come up; I'm not working in the darkroom tonight."

"I can do more than agitate your chemicals," he said, "though I admit I'm becoming an expert at that."

She could see him struggling with a grin and her frown deepened. The truth of the statement was all too apparent

160

in her body's reaction to him. Damn! Why wouldn't he leave? It was hard to keep her resolutions with him so close. Her body was trying to overrule her mind, but Stacy was determined to put up a fight. The possessiveness he'd shown in the newsroom had thoroughly frightened her.

She shrugged and resumed going up the stairs. "I obviously can't pick you up and bodily put you out the door."

Ward followed her to the workroom and looked curiously about him. The wooden floor beneath him creaked faintly when he walked across the room to Stacy, who was leaning against the counter that ran along one entire wall, checking the temperature gauge of the mounting press.

"I told a friend about your darkroom," Ward said. "He was green with envy. He said his oldest kid was wearing his enlarger on her teeth."

"What?"

Ward chuckled. "Just when he's saved up enough money for some equipment, a family crisis strikes and he loses it. It's tough on him with a wife and three kids."

"Well, it wasn't easy without the three kids."

"Do you ever want to have children, Stacy?" he asked softly.

She closed her eyes. Did she? A rueful smile lifted the corners of her mouth. Yes, she wanted children, but not "accidentally," not to patch up a bad marriage, or fill up the void of loneliness.

She wanted a child who could be loved for his or her own sake alone and who would grow up knowing his or herself as a person, not just as an appendage to others. Her smile faded. But how could she have children who would know themselves when she had trouble knowing herself?

Realizing she hadn't answered him, she shrugged and said, "Maybe. Someday."

The tacking iron was hot and she began attaching the mounting tissue to the back of a print with long, even strokes. She turned it over and stared at the picture of Ward at Rhyolite. Why had she chosen to do that print first?

After trimming the edges with the rotary paper cutter, she sat down in front of the mounting jig to measure the exact place to mount the picture. But her eyes kept returning to the face in the picture.

She could feel the real Ward standing close behind her, the heat from his body sending her pulse careening. For a moment, reality was suspended—the impact of the real Ward and the enigmatic look of the Ward in the picture made her wonder how she ever thought she could be around him and remain unaffected.

Her mind returned to the jig. Nonsense! Of course she could. *Then why is your heart beating so fast?* a tiny voice mocked.

The print was finally positioned on the mat board and Stacy put it in the mount press and locked the handle in place. The timer ticked off the seconds; it was the only sound in the room.

When the print was finished, she pulled the still hot picture out of the mount press and gingerly slid it onto a rack to cool.

Stepping back, she ran into Ward and immediately tried to move away from him, but his hands gripped her shoulders and held her. Her back was pressed to his chest, the contact causing a reaction she was trying desperately to suppress.

"I was a fool this afternoon," he whispered, his breath teasing the chestnut hair tucked behind her ear. "When you came into the newsroom, you had such a light in your eyes when you saw me. It's killing me to think I might have extinguished that." His lips tasted her skin just below her ear in a kiss.

His voice flowed over her like a caress. "Tell me that light isn't extinguished. Tell me that flame is only dormant and can be awakened." He turned her to face him and, entranced by him, she made no protest. His fingers lifted her chin.

"Awakened with a kiss . . ." he said, his lips already closing on hers.

It was a gentle kiss, a kiss of warmth rather than fireworks and it was doubly devastating because of that. Ardent passion she could have fought, but not this tender, loving contact. Just as she thought her lips were melting against his, he withdrew them.

The backs of his fingers traced the hollow of her cheek. "In Death Valley I found I just wanted to be near you, watching your spirit come alive. At times I felt we were almost one person, one being who could dare to ride the wind to the limits of our imagination. It was beautiful, Stacy, please don't tell me I've thrown that away."

His voice ended on a thread of a whisper and he kissed her again, deeply, passionately, but in a way that asked her to share his joy. His words and lips had reverberated within her, and she answered his kiss with a fervent desire of her own that she had never intended him to rediscover.

His hands stroked her back to her waist while her fingers were kneading the muscles at the base of his neck with a suppressed urgency she herself would not have recognized.

The warmth in her veins was heating the most distant parts of her body and she felt vibrant and alive. She let her lips tell of her love for him, tell him that the fires had indeed only lain dormant.

Her need for him welled up inside of her and she pulled herself closer to his body, his embrace tightening in response. She could feel the hardness of his muscular thighs pressing into her soft flesh and the burning contact of their bodies continued upward as if their entire bodies were taking part in the kiss.

How could she live without him? How could she survive without these fires burning deep inside her? A feeling of panic fluttered near the edges of her consciousness at the thought of losing him. But an answering coldness crept over her, the bone-chilling coldness of a dark cavern, and soon that fear had overridden the panic.

No, she couldn't let herself be caught again. If she let anyone else have that kind of power over her, her own growth would be forever stunted and incomplete.

Ward must have felt her withdrawal. "Stacy, Stacy," he whispered, covering her face with kisses, "we can have so much."

She reached behind her and gently removed his hands.

"A lot has happened today, and I think I'd like to have some time to myself," she said. Her calm manner was more convincing than an angry declaration, and he backed away.

His eyes were moist and his hand touched her face as if to memorize it. "One day I hope you'll forgive me," he said, his voice ragged, "and run into my arms instead of away from them."

His hand dropped to his side and he walked from the room.

"There!" she said aloud to the empty room, "you've got

what you wanted, happy?" Her cheeks were wet with tears.

She turned off the mount press and put everything else away. The rain had lessened, but she could still hear its steady drone on the windows. It gave the room a hollow sound, a sound like the beat of her heart. Her hand was on the light switch when she ran back to the cooling rack. With the picture of Ward in one hand, she turned out the lights.

The newsroom was busy the next day with the reporters writing stories on the aftereffects of the big storm, and no one had time to notice the subdued Stacy, who quietly gathered testimonials from the Jondaw Valley residents.

She only glanced up from her terminal when a man gripping a newspaper stomped into the newsroom. But he soon had everyone's attention.

"I want to see the reporter who wrote that article!" the rotund man shouted, throwing the paper on Ward's desk and pounding it with his finger. "That's slander! I'll sue! You can't say those things about honest folks and get away with it!"

Ward's face was a mask of controlled anger. He picked up the paper and read the first few lines of the offending article. "Are you this Jericho Smith?"

The man's chins connected with his chest in a deep nod. "I am. I'm the one viciously slandered in that thing you call a newspaper." He shook his finger at the *Monitor* in Ward's hands.

Clancy said, "Libel, you turkey," under his breath but Stacy didn't react. She'd written the article on Jericho Smith and his unscrupulous tactics in buying steers raised by the area's high school students.

Ward stood and looked over the man's shoulder to Stacy. "Why don't we go into my office, Mr. Smith," he said. "I'm sure Mrs. Kemble can answer any of your questions."

It took all her courage to return Ward's look. She knew she couldn't hide all her eyes wanted to say and, unfortunately, Smith saw the unspoken interchange.

"Uh-uh! I know who you're going to be listening to, and it isn't me," he said.

Ward frowned and the others in the newsroom suddenly found pressing stories that needed writing, though they did cast sidelong glances at Stacy.

She could feel herself flushing. Evidently her relationship with Ward hadn't been the big secret she'd thought, and she cursed the weasel Smith for embarrassing them all. Lifting her chin higher, she preceded the two men into the editor's office.

"Now, Mr. Smith," Ward said, "what exactly is your complaint?" He motioned Stacy to his chair behind the desk while he perched on one edge of the oak desktop. She had to stifle a smile at his tactics; they certainly presented a united front against this intruder.

Smith had lost some of his bravado when he lost most of his audience, but he still blustered his way through. "That article makes it sound like I cheat!" he began, and gave them ten minutes of dubious testimony on his trustworthiness.

When he'd finally wound down, Ward asked, "Was there anything in the article—specifically—that was inaccurate?"

More blustering. "You know how you can say things that are true and make them sound crooked."

"They might sound crooked because they are," Stacy

said. A pair of gray eyes held an amused smile for her remark and, again, the sharp-eyed Smith caught the look.

"I knew it; you're not going to give me a chance!" the stout red-faced man said. "I want a retraction! I'm going to see my lawyer. Let's see what Floyd Yarrow will make of you!"

He started to leave, but stopped at the door, a leer directed at Stacy. " 'Course we all know how you got this job." He looked pointedly at Ward, but his bravery deserted him when Ward started toward him. "You'll be hearing from Yarrow!"

The door slammed, but Stacy didn't hear it. At Smith's blatant accusation her face had drained of color and her hands had clenched in her lap. She had to get free of this!

The turnoff to San Francisco was up ahead and Stacy signaled, merging her motorcycle into the far right lane of the freeway. It shouldn't be too much longer before she'd reach her father and stepmother's house. Her father had been very understanding when she'd called him; she'd felt new love and respect for the man who had so patiently waited for his daughter to come to terms with her feelings for him, then accepted her so completely. He'd respected her need to be alone these past years, knowing that she must be the one to make the first move out of her self-imposed isolation.

But now Stacy needed him, and when his quiet voice had told her that he and Fran would welcome her to their home, she knew she would be able to find her answers there. Stacy had never met the woman her father had married after her mother had died; the wedding had been soon after Don's death and Stacy had been too wrapped up in her pain and confusion to take part in her father's joy. Though she'd sent her congratulations and eased her conscience with phone calls, she knew she should have made at least a token visit. Either Fran was a very understanding woman, or Stacy was in for a cold reception. Stacy sighed heavily as the thought of a painful scene with her father and Fran triggered the memory of her last unpleasant meeting with Ward at the *Monitor* yesterday.

"What Smith feels or says doesn't matter," he'd said. "We can still work together."

She was standing by his chair and he was facing her, the desk once again between them. "It isn't what he said that's made me reach this decision, it's that he said it at all," she'd told him. "If he can see something between us, then obviously we're not dealing with this thing as I'd hoped. I have to leave the *Monitor*."

"So you're running away at last," he said. She shrugged and walked toward the door, but a hand on her shoulder stopped her. He tilted her chin and placed a feather kiss on her lips. "There's nothing more I can say. *Au revoir,* my love."

Tears blurred her vision, making it difficult to see the freeway signs as she approached San Francisco.

She eased her motorcycle next to the sidewalk in front of the delightful Victorian house. The house had been painted a pale dusty blue with the gingerbread trim in a rich cream color, the whole effect reminding her of a precious cameo heirloom.

She carefully avoided the beveled glass panels and knocked on the edge of the door. A frilled curtain covered the inside of the door, so she heard rather than saw someone approach the door.

A lump of anxiety formed in her throat and she fought the temptation to turn and run back down the stairs to her bike and leave. As she saw the knob turn, she took a deep breath to calm her fluttering stomach.

"Yes? Wait, are you Stacy? Welcome, child," the slender woman greeted her. Her wide smile and warm brown eyes made Stacy take to her instantly. "I'd recognize those eyes anywhere! Come on in, my dear. Randall and I were just having our breakfast. Your father will be so pleased you're here! Have you eaten?"

A wisp of her shoulder-length white-blond hair had escaped from the clip that held it in a neat queue at the nape of her neck, and she absently brushed it behind her ear as she good-naturedly, but thoroughly, looked Stacy over.

"No, I didn't want to stop," Stacy told her, following the older woman down the exquisitely paneled hallway and through a doorway. Stacy couldn't begin to guess how old this woman might be, but she realized it didn't matter. In her father's telephone calls he'd always sounded happy, and that was all that was important.

She stopped short on the threshold to admire the large windows that formed two of the room's walls and overlooked the side- and backyards where a weathered wood fence enclosed luxuriant green foliage.

"Fran's responsible for most of that," a man's voice told her. She turned and saw a remarkably fit man in his late fifties looking at her with a mixture of affection and wariness in his hazel eyes.

A wide smile lit her face as she ran to him, his arms opening instantly to crush her to him in a hug of reunion. No words were needed to express their joy at seeing each other and more than one pair of hazel eyes were damp with happiness.

"Oh, Daddy, I've missed you so," she said, finally

breaking away. He pulled out a chair for her and the white bamboo creaked as she sat down on the cushion covered in bright green windowpane checks.

"I've missed you too, honey," he said. Lines of concern creased his forehead. "Are you okay? That's all I'm going to ask; you can tell us the rest later, if you want to. Right now you need a good breakfast and a chance to relax."

She nodded that she was fine; all the damage was internal anyway. But she was grateful to him for not demanding a full explanation.

He smiled at her and added, "I hope you'll stay as long as you like. Fran's a fantastic hostess." He looked at his wife and Stacy saw the love their eyes exchanged.

She sighed in relief. She had found a sanctuary.

Two hours later she wasn't sure if she could ever find peace. Her father had left for his office and her stepmother had retired to her studio. Fran was a water-colorist of considerable renown, but Stacy had a suspicion that she was working this morning more out of desire to give her stepdaughter time alone than from a pressing need to work. And Stacy didn't want to be alone.

She tried to tour the house as Fran had suggested, but every wall looked out at her with mesmerizing gray eyes, every silent room cried out endearments in Ward's deep spine-teasing voice.

In an attempt to escape him, she fled to the small garden. There, she walked barefoot on the low ground cover, and then sat on the rim of the stone fountain in the corner. It had been turned off for the winter, so the small statue of Neptune had no water to guard. She idly played with the dried leaves that it had captured from a nearby tree. The angular features of the man still haunted her.

170

The back door slamming shut made her jerk upright; she couldn't let anyone see her like this! Putting on a bright smile, and turning toward the sound, she was surprised to feel the dampness on her cheeks. She impatiently dashed away the tears with the back of her hand.

"Thought you might want some lunch," Fran said, carrying a tray with sandwiches. She set it down between them, and Stacy realized how hungry she was.

Between bites, her stepmother said, "Randall tells me you're a photographer. I'd like to see some of your work, were you able to bring any with you?"

"I brought a few pieces in a portfolio that I tied to the seat behind me," Stacy answered. "But the bulk of my work is back in Hannah."

After lunch Stacy spread the ten matted prints out on the table in her stepmother's studio. The northern light from the windows gave her pictures a subtle depth.

Fran was quiet for a long time, studying one print and then the next without comment. The last one was the one of Ward, and Stacy held her breath when the older woman studied it the longest.

Her stepmother picked the print up and, taking down a water color from an easel, set the picture on display. Ward stared out at Stacy in the studio's light.

"This man is special to you, isn't he?" Fran asked softly. At Stacy's startled look, she pointed to the print. "That look in his eyes tells me he cares a great deal for you. Men have that certain expression only when they love—and trust—someone very much. And that emotion he feels for you has been reflected in the care you took with the print."

"But I made the others with the same care!" Stacy protested.

"The same technical care, I'll agree," Fran said, "but

see how the texture of the rocky ground surface is so crisp you can almost feel it crunching beneath his feet. And here, this wall could so easily have been a featureless white, glaring mass, but you've managed to bring out the subtle tones of the weather-worn stone. It's superb, Stacy."

With an uneven smile of thanks Stacy turned back to the other prints and began gathering them up.

"No, wait, dear," Fran said, squeezing her stepdaughter's shoulder affectionately. "Haven't you wondered why a woman who dabbles in water colors would be judging photographs?"

"I assumed all the arts have some common standard of what makes them good," Stacy answered.

"That's true, to a point, but it's really because the gallery where I show my work also shows photography," her stepmother said. "In fact, I'd like to take these down there right now to show César. Arouet's gallery has an extensive photographic print collection; it's not too avant garde, mind you, but it has a good, solid reputation."

Putting a piece of tissue paper between the last two prints, Stacy zipped up the portfolio. She mulled her stepmother's offer over. Her work was good—she had to believe that or she wouldn't keep doing it—but good enough for a gallery? And a San Francisco gallery at that?

"If you're doing it because the work is good, and not just because you're married to my father, I'll do it," she said, deciding that the only way to know if her work was good enough for a gallery was to take it to one.

Fran smiled. "I'm delighted, my dear," she said, giving Stacy another squeeze. "But I do take my profession seriously. I looked at your work because you're Randall's daughter; I'm recommending it to César because you're a fine photographer."

Fran walked toward the phone on the wall. "Let me phone him to make sure he's free."

"I still can't believe it!" Stacy cried, giving Fran an impetuous hug as they left the gallery. "Did he really take seven of my prints? Pinch me, I must be dreaming!"

Her stepmother laughed and lightly pinched Stacy's arm. "Yes, my dear, he did." Her brown eyes searched Stacy's face before she said, "César wanted to take eight prints, you know. Why wouldn't you let him hang the best of them?"

Stacy avoided meeting Fran's concerned gaze. "I just thought a portrait wouldn't fit in among all those landscapes," she said softly. How could she tell her stepmother that one didn't hang one's heart on the wall of a gallery?

CHAPTER TEN

A week and a half later, Monsieur Arouet called to congratulate Stacy—two of her prints had been sold and several other patrons had expressed interest in her work. Had she enough material for a show?

After she hung up, Stacy wondered why she had agreed to a show in six months time. She would have been ecstatic at the offer when she'd been in Death Valley, or even a few weeks ago in her darkroom. But now she meandered around the house with her hands in her pockets and her camera upstairs in her bedroom.

Stacy finally went out to the fountain. The tiny garden had become a favorite place of hers—she would sit on the edge of the stone basin, thinking and musing.

"Oh, there you are!" Fran said, walking toward her. After a concerned glance at her stepdaughter, the woman continued. "I need to go out for a bit—will you be all right?" Her brown eyes darted back to the house apprehensively, then back at Stacy. "Why don't you have lunch in the solarium? That might cheer you up."

"Thanks, Fran," Stacy answered, "that sounds inviting."

"I don't have to leave just now, if you'd rather I stayed."

"Now, why would you want to do that? I'm a big girl," Stacy said with an affectionate smile. "And I'm just sitting out here thinking—the best times of my vacations are when I can be lazy and not do anything." She felt guilty for the white lie, but though her father and Fran knew she was troubled, Stacy knew how solicitous they would be if she'd told them she'd quit her job. And all she wanted was quiet and time to think.

"If you're sure . . ." Seeing Stacy's nod, she gave the house one more glance, and then slipped out the side gate and was gone.

When she was alone, a bird flew down and settled on the top of Neptune's head.

"Looking for something, are you?" The tiny head tilted to one side as if trying to understand her words. "Sorry, little one, but I have nothing for you. Nothing at all." Her voice caught on her last words.

"Come on, Stace! Get a hold of yourself," she cried aloud, tilting her face up to the late morning sun to blink away the tears. The movement startled the bird and she watched it fly up into the highest boughs of the nearby tree.

She brushed the crumbled leaves from her lap and stood up. Going into the kitchen, she spied the bright sourdough bread wrapper and her mouth started watering. Rummaging in the refrigerator, she cut herself a good-sized wedge of cheddar cheese and poured a tumbler of iced tea.

Stuffing the large chunk of bread into her mouth to carry it, and holding the cheese in one hand and her tea in the other, she leaned on the swinging door to the solarium to open it. After a stunned look inside, she turned around and went back into the kitchen, dropping her lunch on the counter.

How did he get here? Why was he here? Hearing a tiny squeak, she turned toward the door in panic. No! He can't come in here! But Ward's tall dark frame didn't appear in the doorway. Relief at realizing that he hadn't followed her quickly turned to pique.

She looked again at the door to the solarium. "Well, this is as far as the chase goes, Mr. Fallbrook," she whispered to the room.

Taking a deep breath to steady her nerves, she took two long strides toward the door, and hesitating at it only briefly, pushed it open.

"Ward, why are you here?" she asked as soon as she entered the room, her hands on her hips. He was standing in the corner of the windows, looking out over the garden and, with an unpleasant start, she realized that he must have been watching her. Her frown deepened. Now she understood Fran's glances toward the house; naturally, her stepmother had known he was here.

The gray eyes reflected an inner turmoil. "Stacy. Marry me." He said nothing more, and did not approach her. But he leaned forward, his finely formed hands clutching the back of a white bamboo chair and his fingers wrapping themselves around the intricate pattern.

"Why are you doing this to me?" she cried. "I don't understand you . . ."

"I love you," he said quietly.

Being in the small room with him was doing things to her senses. She couldn't think; her mind was insisting on recalling all the comfort and warmth she'd found in his arms.

"Stacy, at least let's talk about it," he said. "We've never seriously discussed what it is that bothers you about marriage and commitment."

Her eyes searched his face and saw only his love and sincerity. "I—I—I'm not sure what to do," she said, her fingers stroking her temple. What he said was true; she'd been the one wary of talking about feelings and emotions. She'd thought that wrapping herself up tightly in an emotional cocoon would protect her. But even then she hadn't been free from pain.

He released his grip on the chair and closed the space between them, yet he still didn't touch her. "I'm not Don," he said. "I don't think like him, I don't react like him, but I think I do have one thing he didn't . . ."

She looked up from studying the pattern on the chair's cushion, her hazel eyes questioning.

His silver gaze held hers and his hand came up to stroke her cheek. "I have Stacy Kemble's love."

Her features registered her shock, but she couldn't bring herself to deny his words. His presence was forcing her to a decision she didn't want to make and her mind started to resist the urging of her heart.

"You don't listen when I say no or tell you to leave me alone. What good will still another scene do?"

"Give me one day—tomorrow. I know my coming here has been a shock to you, so I'll leave for today. But only if you say you'll meet me tomorrow."

"Where? Not here."

"I'm not that familiar with San Francisco. Fisherman's Wharf?" he said cautiously, his eyes telling her he was struggling to not let her see the hope there.

"No, too many people," she said, frowning. She had begun to realize that this meeting would decide the course of her life. "How about the Palace of the Legion of Honor? It's a museum; the grounds are beautiful and few people go there in the middle of the week." He nodded and she added, "I could meet you there about ten tomorrow morning in the courtyard."

"I'll be there," he told her. "And I think you've realized I'm not going to give you up easily. I love you too much."

She left her BMW in the fine-art museum's parking lot and walked down between the two long collonades past the Rodin sculpture, the soles of her casual running shoes silent on the concrete.

"You're early," Ward said, turning from his contemplation of Rodin's famous "Thinker" in the palace's courtyard. He smiled when he noticed her dark blue denim jeans and lavender jacket over a purple and lavender print blouse. "I was afraid you'd arrived dressed to the hilt. That would've been a bad sign for me. Do you want to go inside, or just walk around?"

"Let's just walk around for a while," she said. "Why would my being dressed up have been a bad sign?" She didn't mention her vacillation between a white linen suit with a green silk blouse and the outfit she ended up wearing.

"For as long as I've know you, you get dressed up only when you either think you have to or when you want to hide behind formality." He too was wearing jeans, less new than hers, and one of his favorite striped cotton shirts, the long sleeves rolled up to his elbows.

They settled on a grassy knoll and silently watched the churning Pacific where it entered San Francisco Bay.

She felt his eyes on her and she turned from the steel gray of the water. "I was going to come here and tell you I'd changed my mind and didn't want to talk to you. But I've run from you once too often. I'll listen to what you have to say."

"Besides, I love you and want to marry you?"

"Besides that," she said, smiling.

He stretched out on the grass next to her, his head on his propped-up hand. "I'd rather listen to what you have to say."

"Me? I'd thought I'd said too much already," Stacy said, hugging her knees to her.

"You've told me about your marriage to Don, but I don't think that's a barrier between us anymore. Is it?"

She shook her head. "No, I've exorcised that pain. I never thought you would act like him, but the awful suffocation that I felt with him would well up inside of me and all I could do was escape the cause."

"I was the cause?"

"A couple of times. When I came back from the dam, for one," she said.

He turned onto his back and closed his eyes, his hands folded under his head. "I did act stupidly there, but, God, I was terrified something had happened to you. Every time I would imagine what could have happened, I would die a little inside. And I tried to apologize—several times."

"I realize now that it was far from normal behavior for you," she said. She let her gaze wander over the man next to her and smiled. "I also realize that had I stayed with you five years ago, we'd have parted company not long after."

He sat up quickly and faced her. "Why on earth would you say that?"

"You mentioned the reason up at the lookout in Death Valley, but I didn't want to face it then. Now I understand."

"Your mother," he said immediately.

She nodded slowly. "I was scared I would end up like

she did; I didn't realize that that was the way she was. I talked to my Dad last night—he said sometimes he regretted that I was so bright, it had seemed natural to tell me his troubles. Hindsight has changed his perspective."

"And now . . ." he prompted.

"These past two weeks have been wonderful," she said. Seeing his rueful smile, she added, "Not that I'd want to go through them again, but they have been a revelation to me. Dad and Fran are truly happy together. Even when they argue over something, there's this sense of 'of course we'll work it out.' "

He took her hand in his, his thumb tracing the outline of her fingers. "A man and a woman who love each other can have a good life together; it's not idyllic, not a fairytale life where everything's in soft focus, but a life of sharing and coping and feeling whole." His thumb was circling the palm of her hand. "I want that kind of life with you."

Fear tightened her stomach. "Can you . . . can you give me just a little more time?" The expression on his face made her add quickly, "Not days, just a few hours. It's one thing to understand these changes intellectually, but another to come to grips with my less than rational fears. I need just a little while longer."

"I'm starving," he said, standing and holding out his hand to her to help her up.

He understood; he was giving her time. "There are some fantastic seafood restaurants on Fisherman's Wharf," she said, smiling. "How about sharing a huge pot of cioppino?"

In the parking lot Ward grinned at her sudden frown when she realized he would once again have to ride behind her on the motorcycle. That was not the way to let herself think things through coolly and rationally. But taking a taxi would have been ridiculous.

He sat on the bike first and waited for her to join him. Stalling for time, she snapped on her helmet and spent several moments adjusting it until Ward crossed his arms over his chest, his smile telling her he recognized her tactics.

She got on in front of him and sat down on the seat, a gasp escaping her when her body touched his. His hard, muscled chest was pressed into her back and his arms encircled her waist.

"Could we take a short side trip first?" he asked, his breath teasing her exposed neck. "I've never been down Lombard Street."

She smiled back and him and nodded. The beat of her pulse was a physical sensation, throbbing in her neck and body with an undeniable passion.

Lombard Street. She fumbled with the map, trying to locate the crooked street while Ward shifted slightly to look over her shoulder. The increased contact only added to the urgency in her blood and it was several minutes before she spotted the zigzag line that indicated the street.

She memorized her route, then headed out, taking deep gulps of air to counteract the growing need within her. She had to have all her wits about her to drive in San Francisco traffic, but Ward's hands exploring her waist and sides were making it difficult to concentrate.

Naturally there had to be a stop sign at the top of the hill! Stacy clamped down the brakes, hoping they would hold, and was grateful when Ward put his feet on the ground to steady the bike.

Gripping the throttle, she said, "Hold on, the corners are really tight." She could feel Ward grin behind her as she felt his arms tighten about her even more. His entire body was pressed into hers, burning an unbreakable bond between them.

The sensations his body were causing increased as they descended the switchbacks of the street. She tilted the bike and leaned into each turn, and Ward did the same, his body moving against hers. Fortunately the crooked part only lasted for a long block.

But Ward held her close until they arrived at Fisherman's Wharf, making her acknowledge that time could not extinguish the fire flaming inside.

They spent the rest of the day seeing the sights of the beautiful city and Stacy almost regretted it when she pulled up in front of her father's house.

"Let's walk for a minute," Ward said, taking her elbow and guiding her up the street. It was nearing dusk and the city's lights spread out below them as they walked to the crest of the hill.

"I'm only human," he said. "I can't wait any longer."

"I don't need any more time, Ward." She'd reached her decision, and though it frightened her, she was prepared to live with the risk.

They stopped at the top of the hill and he held her shoulders in an unconsciously tight grip. "Will you, Stacy? Will you make that commitment and marry me?"

The tip of her finger traced the edge of his jaw. She drew it over his lips and said, "Yes."

She felt the tension go out of his body and he crushed her to him, his voice thick and ragged.

"Oh, God, you don't know how empty I've been without you." His lips found hers and he left her in no doubt of his passion and love.

"I love you," she whispered. "I've always loved you. It

terrified me, but after seeing Dad and Fran, I realized it was worth the risk."

"Why did you wait to answer me?" he asked softly, his eyes never leaving his love's face. His fingers stroked her neck, reveling in the silken touch of her.

"My heart knew, but I had to convince the rest of me that marriage with you would be wonderful."

He smiled and kissed her forehead. "I knew all along that marriage with you would be wonderful—and exciting, exasperating, challenging, and thoroughly satisfying."

"Anything else?" she asked with a laugh.

"Umm-hmm," he said, nibbling her neck, "and terrific in—" His mouth closed over hers, his lips explaining what words would never be able to say.

When they broke apart, they stood absorbed by their love and happiness. Secure in the rightness of their coming life together, they walked back to her father's house, his arm across her shoulder and her arm around his waist.

The ceremony took place in the garden with Neptune overlooking the proceedings, along with Stacy's father and stepmother. The celebratory luncheon was held in the solarium, the golden sunlight and the rich green of the plants reflected in the bride's love-filled eyes.

Later she went up to pack and Ward followed her. "There are so many things we haven't discussed!" she said, folding up a blouse and tucking it into a saddlebag.

"For instance?" he asked.

"Would you mind moving from your apartment into my house? I know the landlord wouldn't mind . . ."

The tenderness in his gaze had become a decided twinkle. "Oh, did I forget?" He reached into his pocket and pulled out a folded piece of paper. "Best wishes on your wedding, ma'am," he said with a grin.

"The deed to the house? But you said you weren't at all sure I would marry you!"

"I wasn't. I thought if I couldn't be your husband, I could at least be your landlord."

"You weren't going to give up, were you!" she said with a laugh. "How could you be so sure I wouldn't move out?"

"I was relying on your darkroom to hold you there," he said. "Remember that fellow I said I'd talked to?"

"The one with the kid wearing braces?"

"Right. He was practically drooling when I told him about your set-up. He said it sounded perfect for a photographer and if he'd had a set-up like that, fires, floods, and earthquakes couldn't keep him away from it."

"You were probably right; I would have been very reluctant to leave it," she said, the light of laughter in her eyes being replaced by uncertainty. "Which brings up another point. About my job . . ."

"You want it back?"

"No, not exactly," she said, biting her lower lip. "I told you a gallery here in San Francisco has accepted some of my work." He nodded. "Well, actually, I'm also going to have a show in six months and I need time to get ready. I've saved some money, so I won't be a financial burden, but the thing is, I don't want my job back. Being a photographer isn't all that lucrative, but it's what I want to do."

He hugged her to him. "A show! Why didn't you tell me before? Of course you can't go back to being a reporter," he said, his breath warm in her hair. "In fact, I was going to suggest that you become a full-time photographer. After seeing you in Death Valley, I knew there could be no other job for you. That and . . ."

She looked up at him. "And what? Didn't you think I was a good reporter?"

"You're a fantastic reporter," he said, smiling, "but you're an even better photographer. Those shots you took at the Jondaw reservoir have been nominated for a state-wide award."

"Really?"

"Really," he said, dropping a kiss her on her nose. "But why didn't you tell me about your show? I don't want to start our relationship with one of us reluctant to confide in the other. With us, it has to be give and take all the way."

"Before you arrived, having that show was the only direction I could see my life taking. But when you appeared, I suddenly thought I'd have to choose between you and the show," she said, and the furrows of thought cleared from her brow. "Now I know I can have both my loves—you and photography. Though you do have slight priority," she added with an impish smile.

"Your smiles are irresistible." He pulled her to him in a kiss of promise and joy.

Breaking away, he said, "By the way, hadn't we better get moving? We have a way to go before dark." His sparkling eyes told her what they were going to be doing after dark.

"I'm almost packed," she said, returning to the clothes on the bed.

At the door her father gave her a kiss and a fierce bear hug. "I wish you all happiness," he said. Fran embraced them, her eyes moist, though she'd vowed she never cried at weddings.

When they were standing on the front steps, Stacy

185

looked at her motorcycle and had to blink. Was she seeing double?

There, parked next to hers, was another 650 BMW. Ward said, "You got me hooked. Though after riding through San Francisco with you, I'm not so sure two bikes are a good thing. I didn't mind the passenger seat at all, as long as you're the driver."

Touched by his gesture, she hugged him impulsively, "Oh, Ward, I do love you!" Their lips met in a kiss.

"I'd love to continue this conversation," he said, his mouth hovering over hers. "But not on the front porch of your father's house."

"It doesn't take that long to get to Hannah." She giggled and kissed him again.

"Now it's my vacation," he said, "and I'm going to Mendocino." His lips slid across hers in another kiss, the sparks of desire shooting through her body, but when she would have deepened the kiss, he drew back. "You're welcome to come along. . . ."

With their motorcycles side by side, they crossed the Golden Gate Bridge, heading for the northern California coast. Smiling, Stacy turned to look toward him. He'd put his visor up; his mouth moved, and though she couldn't hear the words, she could read his lips saying "I love you."

She threw him a kiss. Her attention returned to the road ahead, but her smile remained.

Come Faith, Come Fire

Vanessa Royall

Proud as her aristocratic upbringing, bold as the ancient gypsy blood that ran in her veins, the beautiful golden-haired Maria saw her family burned at the stake and watched her young love, forced into the priesthood. Desperate and bound by a forbidden love, Maria defies the Grand Inquisitor himself and flees across Spain to a burning love that was destined to be free! $2.95